2

STORY BY
Hirukuma

ILLUSTRATION BY
Ituwa Kato

D0061627

Reborn as a
VendingMachine,
------ I Now Wander the
DUNGEON

"You get to sleep with two beautiful women. Best night ever, right?"

Hulemy

"Yup. Okay, let's go to sleep! Oh, Boxxo, you can sleep in our tent tonight."

Lammis

"None of this is your fault. This time, you can rest in peace."

Reborn as a Vending Machine, I Now Wander the DUNGEON

2

Hirukuma

ILLUSTRATION BY
Ituwa Kato

YEN
ON

NEW YORK

Reborn as a Uending Machine, I Now Wander the Dungeon

VOLUME 2

Hirukuma

Translation by Andrew Prowse
Cover art by Ituwa Kato

This book is a work of fiction. Names, characters, places, and incidents are the product of the author's imagination or are used fictitiously. Any resemblance to actual events, locales, or persons, living or dead, is coincidental.

JIDOU HANBAIKI NI UMAREKAWATTA ORE HA MEIKYUU WO SAMAYOU, Vol. 2
© 2016 Hirukuma, Ituwa Kato
First published in Japan in 2016 by KADOKAWA CORPORATION, Tokyo.
English translation rights arranged with KADOKAWA CORPORATION, Tokyo, through
TUTTLE-MORI AGENCY, INC., Tokyo.

Yen On
1290 Avenue of the Americas
New York, NY 10104

Visit us at yenpress.com

facebook.com/yenpress yenpress.tumblr.com
twitter.com/yenpress instagram.com/yenpress

First Yen On Edition: August 2018

Yen On is an imprint of Yen Press, LLC.
The Yen On name and logo are trademarks of Yen Press, LLC.

Library of Congress Cataloging-in-Publication Data
Names: Hirukuma, author. | Kato, Ituwa, illustrator. | Prowse, Andrew (Andrew R.), translator.
Title: Reborn as a vending machine, I now wander the dungeon / Hirukuma ;
illustration by Ituwa Kato ; translation by Andrew Prowse.
Other titles: Jidou hanbaiki ni umarekawatta ore wa meikyuu wo samayou. English
Description: First Yen On edition. | New York, NY : Yen On, April 2018–
Identifiers: LCCN 2018004692 | ISBN 9780316479110 (v. 1 : pbk.) |
ISBN 9780316479134 (v. 2 : pbk.)
Classification: LCC PL871.I77 J5313 2018 | DDC 895.63/6—dc23
LC record available at https://lccn.loc.gov/2018004692

ISBNs: 978-0-316-47913-4 (paperback)
978-0-316-47914-1 (ebook)

1 3 5 7 9 10 8 6 4 2

LSC-C

Printed in the United States of America

Reborn as a Vending Machine, I Now Wander the DUNGEON

CONTENTS

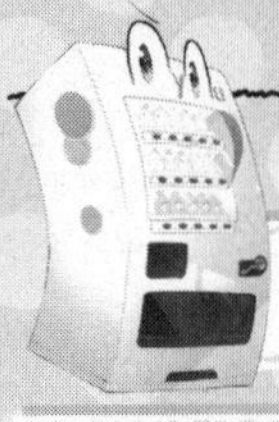

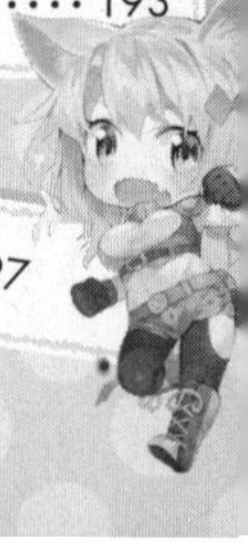

Characters

Boxxo

A former vending machine maniac.
He can sell any product he bought from a
vending machine in his past life.

Lammis

An energetic, sprightly, incredibly strong girl.
Has more power than she knows what to
do with. Boxxo's partner.

Hulemy

A talented magic-item engineer. Lammis's childhood friend; behaves like her older sister.

Shirley

Runs a business of the night.
A cordial person.

Director Bear

Director of the Hunters Association.
Deeply considerate of the people.

Suori

Daughter of a tycoon. Selfish and strong-willed
but a little interested in Boxxo.

Prologue

"This weather's great."

I broke a desk when I tried to help clean the house, and Ma got mad at me, but that's okay! The sky is blue, the air is sweet, and the water is beautiful. There's no time for feeling down.

What should I do today? I tried to help Pa with his farm work, but I broke the machine, and he smiled and said I didn't have to do anything, so…I guess I'll go fishing.

They get mad at me whenever I wander outside of the village, but it should be fine if I just stick to the wall.

"Well, if it isn't Lammis. Where are you off to play today?"

"Um, I'm going to look at the flowers!"

"Is that right? Well, just be sure not to leave the village, okay? Recently, I've been hearing about neighboring villages getting attacked by monsters."

"Don't talk to children about that, dear. Be careful, Lammis."

"I will!"

My aunt and uncle who live next door are field workers. They would've definitely gotten mad at me if I told them the truth, so I lied. The river is just outside the wall, so I'm sure I'll be fine.

I usually get caught if I use the large path, so let's try a route people don't normally take.

This should be good. I can go behind the houses, all the way to the wall. It's perfect!

"Hey, Lammis! What're you doing?"

"*H-hyaa!* I…I'm sorry! I know what I did ain't right, but, um—uh, hold up; just go 'head and forget I said anything!"

The jig is up. If Pa and Ma find out about this, they'll be super mad.

"Pfft, ha-ha-ha-ha. Your accent always comes out whenever you're excited."

Wait, that laugh—it's Hulemy!

"Oh, for cryin' out loud! Don't scare me like that! I thought my heart was gonna jump right outta my chest!"

"Sorry, sorry."

Hulemy, my best friend ever, grinned at me, her frizzy light-brown hair fluttering.

I like exercise and hate studying, but Hulemy is the opposite. She reads hard books and makes all kinds of things. The adults ask her to fix their tools for them. The village relies on her, even though she's a kid. She's amazing.

I don't know my own strength, so I'm always breaking things, but Hulemy never complains. She just fixes them for me.

She talks sort of like a boy, and she's aggressive, too. I've never seen her lose an argument. I always hear the boys whispering about her, calling her *boss*, but I won't tell her that.

"Anyway, where are you sneaking off to?"

"Well, I was going to go to the river…"

"The river? You're going outside? You can't get out without climbing over the wall. They won't let kids through the gate."

The log wall is a lot bigger than I am, but I can make it if I jump really hard. Then again, if I use too much strength and break the wall, they'll get super mad at me again.

"No, there's a hole in part of the wall. Adults can't get through, but I can."

"Oh, really? I didn't know about that. In that case, I'll tag along."

"Well, that's fine, but…keep it a secret."

"Sure thing. I promise."

Hulemy never breaks her promises. I'll be fine. Yup.

Behind the houses, we're hidden by the shadows of trees, so anyone nearby can't see us. Let's see—I just have to move this big rock out of the way.

"Whoa. There really *is* a hole here."

"Yup. The big rock is in the way, so I don't think you can get in from outside."

"A 'rock'... Lammis, that's a boulder. This isn't some ordinary secret passage. Nobody could move that thing."

Is it really that surprising? The rock is bigger than a grown-up, but grown-ups could move it, too.

"Okay," I say. "You go first, Hulemy. I have to put the rock back afterward."

"Make sure you cover the hole up, got it?"

"Yup. Wouldn't want anyone coming in." Ma always tells me that it's important to close the door behind me.

As we go through the hole in the wall, we see the familiar forest and river. Maybe I'll catch some fish today.

"Whoa. A shortcut directly opposite the gate? Talk about convenient. I guess you can't use it unless Lammis is around, though." Hulemy folds her arms and thinks.

This is my secret hangout, but it's okay because we're friends.

Let's see. Should we play in the water first? Or pick flowers first? Hmm... What to do, what to do?

"Hey, did you just hear a shout from the village?"

"They didn't find out, did they?!"

If they did, they'll yell at me again. What now? If I go right back and say sorry, will they forgive me?

"I don't know. It sounded pretty angry."

"Oh no... U-um, let's catch some fish and go back! I'm sure they'll forgive us then...maybe?"

"They probably would go easy on us if we brought back a gift or something."

Yeah. They'll be happy if we bring back extra food for lunch.

Okay. We just have to catch as many as we can and then go home.

"Let's get to it, then."

"Fishing, huh?" says Hulemy. "Hang on a minute. I'll make a pole with branches and ivy."

"What? I can catch fish with my hands."

I walk into the river shallows, then throw a punch at some fish in the water. The river water makes a slapping noise as it splashes, and the fish splash up with it.

Three of them fly out; two land back in the water, but one falls onto the gravel.

"The force of your fist sent everything flying, fish and all..."

"See? I caught one."

Hulemy's eyes are really wide, like she's surprised. Did I do something wrong?

Oh, I know. Mom says I have to be careful, since I'm too strong, and that makes me different from other people. It makes me different from the other kids, too.

"Sorry for startling you..."

"Yeah, that was a fright! But it's just as I thought. You're awesome, Lammis!"

"Huh? But I'm too strong, so I always break things, and people get mad at me a lot, and the boys make fun of me and call me a monster...," I say, starting to feel sad as I say it. I wish I was cuter. All I ever do is scare people.

"What the heck are you talking about? Being strong is an amazing talent. I'm telling you, one day, that strength is going to come in handy. One day, you'll be glad you have it! I'm sure of it!"

Isn't Hulemy scared?

Why is she saying nice things to me? I break things in the house, I can't do anything right, and Pa gives me a smile that makes me feel like a bother.

"Chin up! If you keep your head down like that, you can't choose what you want to buy."

"Buy?"

What is she talking about? Buy... Huh?!

Wait, where did Hulemy go? What's this big squarish box? It wasn't here a minute ago. Where did it come from?

A lot of pretty things are lined up inside. It's like a treasure chest. What should I do with it?

"Welcome."

Wait, I heard a voice. Could it be…? "Did you talk?"

This box, I…I know what it is. Um, where did we meet, again?

When I touch it, it's hard and cold, but for some reason, I feel relieved.

I know this touch… The one always beside me, protecting my back… That's right, I remember now.

How could I have forgotten something so important?

This big, kind, rectangular box is a precious magic item that saved my life—Boxxo.

Together with You

"Boxxo... Don't be leavin' me again..."

Ever since we were rescued from the underground room, we've been resting in a corner of the fortress. Lammis, all her tension melted away, had leaned against me and fallen asleep.

After I disappeared, she must have been searching for me around the clock without much sleep.

"Lammis depends on you quite a bit, huh? The way she's so bent out of shape... This must have reminded her of what happened back then."

Back then? Hulemy just piqued my interest. "Too bad."

"Right, you don't know what I'm talking about. Well, I guess I can tell you. Lammis and me are from the same village. Childhood friends, and all that."

I see. They seem like polar opposites, but they do say people with opposing personalities get along surprisingly well.

"Anyway, it's a common story. A small, nameless village, wiped out by a monster attack. Lammis and me are among its few survivors... Well, in any case, both her parents died."

I've always thought Lammis's words and actions were kind of infantile, and that she needed attention. Maybe she's been subconsciously seeking someone to depend on—a substitute for her parents.

"As for me—well, I can handle myself, but ever since then, she's regretted being unable to do anything besides cowering in fear despite having the strength to make a difference when it counts. She was always a slow-witted girl who wouldn't hurt a fly. But now she's gone and become a hunter? Idiot."

Her words were sharp, but her voice was full of concern.

Lammis's Might certainly fit the bill for hunters, but I'll be honest: She's not cut out for fighting. When she's working at her inn job or helping clear debris, she looks like she's truly enjoying herself. If I could, I'd tell her to give up the dangerous hunting life.

But she feels strongly about this. She has a reason she can't give it up. I'd like to help her if I could, but...

"Boxxo, do you have a moment?"

"Welcome."

Oh, Director Bear is here, too? At a glance, the raid on this base consisted of around ten members, and I can see the Menagerie of Fools among them. Their captain and vice captain are keeping an eye on me as they take a rest.

"Lammis is asleep? The exhaustion must have gotten to her. Let her sleep for a while, then. I must apologize for this incident. I had received prior information revealing that this band of thieves was after you. Tomorrow, I had planned to request that you act as a decoy to round up the whole lot at once, but then things got out of hand. Still, we should have helped you, but at my orders, we decided to tail you instead. This may have been to corner the thieves, but it still put you in danger. You have my apologies."

Director Bear bowed deeply before me. That was about what I'd figured, so I was neither shocked nor indignant. In hindsight, their non-intervention in my kidnapping allowed me to meet and subsequently save Hulemy.

If they hadn't kidnapped me, there's no telling what might have happened to her. Nobody needs to be sorry for anything.

"Welcome."

"In light of the trouble this incident has caused you, you shall be rewarded for your efforts. Additionally, should anything happen to you in the future, Boxxo, I promise you that the Hunters Association will spare no effort in lending you our aid."

The simple fact that I now have a powerful link to Director Bear is more than enough reward.

"Geez, let us go already. Are you bastards really just gonna swipe all the loot I've hoarded?!"

That angry shout must have come from their boss. I look over and see them all bound up in ropes. One of them lay on his side unmoving—a corpse. He was the lookout. Despite seeing a dead human body, it isn't shocking, or even a little disturbing.

"What's this? More worried about your money than your life? You seem awfully calm about all this. Don't worry—the Hunters Association will put these piles of money to good use."

His fingers tracing the brim of his hat, Captain Kerioyl speaks to them slowly and loosely, rubbing at his sleepy-looking eyes.

I'm glad to be rescued, but now I'm indebted to the Menagerie of Fools. I've got a bad feeling about this. By the way, Captain, most of the coins they hoarded are inside me now. Though if he knew that, he'd probably be upset.

Anyway, whatever the case may be, the kidnapping affair has come to an end. Now Lammis and I just have to wait for morning and go home, with me nestled comfortably on her back.

Now, then! I think it's time to reward the hardworking hunters with a lavish feast. Since I have a new mode to heat up frozen food, I can sell grilled rice balls, *karaage* fried chicken, french fries, fried rice, fried soba noodles (or *yakisoba*), and even fried octopus dumplings known as *takoyaki*. It's all from a vending machine manufacturer that's also famous for their frozen foods, so it'll all taste good, guaranteed.

Personally, I recommend the *karaage*.

"Oh hey, Boxxo changed shape. And what are these new food pictures? They look great!"

"I've never seen any of this stuff before!"

"All of you, calm down. They could be dangerous, you know. Let me, the captain, be the first to try them."

"No fair, no fair! Captain, that's no fair!"

"You're a tyrant! Organizations that don't value their subordinates never see any new blood!"

As Captain Kerioyl pushes through the line of hunters in front of me, the Menagerie members cling to him, stopping him from moving.

"Ahhh, dammit. I'm docking your pay, all of you!"

"What lunacy is this? Boxxo, there appear to be no prices displayed beneath any of these items. Could it be that you're treating us?"

"Welcome."

"Thank you very much. Then I will have this meat lump."

Filmina, the vice captain, ignores the captain and crew as they goof around and pushes the button for *karaage*.

"Thank you."

"H-hey, Filmina, you can't just waltz on up ahead of us!"

"Vice Captain Filmina, that's not fair!"

"This meat is almost unbelievably soft. When I bite into it, all the juices come flowing out... Ahh..."

Robbed of her stoic demeanor, Vice Captain Filmina puts her hand to her cheek and breaks into a smile. The other hunters, seeing her blissful expression, all at once run out of patience. Their hands extend toward me, one after the next.

All right, all right, you don't need to fight over me. Everyone can have as much food and drink as they want. I can't provide any alcohol, but I can give you everything else.

"You've got all these people flocking to you. They look so happy. Any person would have a hard time pulling this off," says Hulemy, her black outfit curiously closed in the front, as she raps her knuckles on my body. Though it was a casual remark, I feel a warm sensation. Maybe I don't have actual senses like that, since I have a mechanical body, but I want to believe this feeling, this warmth, isn't just my imagination.

As the hunters continue to eat and drink, I'm simply happy to provide. This sensation is less a sprouting of my self-awareness as a vending machine and more natural human emotion. As long as I can hang on to these feelings and values, I can press on as a vending machine, come what may.

"Boxxo... Let's be...together...forever...zzz."

Lammis is curled up in slumber like a kitten, wearing a blissful expression on her face.

Okay. Until the day comes when you're the one to leave me, let's be together.

*　　*　　*

We arrived back at the settlement without any accidents on the way.

Karios and Gorth, the two gatekeepers, are there to welcome me safely back from the hideout, overjoyed as though they were the ones that had been rescued. When we went back to the Hunters Association after that, customers began coming out of the woodwork. It became such a crowd that I couldn't see my surroundings.

It would seem that going even one day without tasting my products proved too much for some; many people buy much more than usual. As I gaze over the lines of customers, I glimpse Miss Acowi, the money changer, with a suspicious glint in her eyes.

She's scribbling something into a notebook. She must mean to retrieve the silver coins I've accumulated so many of.

Despite the fact that I had returned early in the morning, the lines of customers didn't disperse until nighttime. It was practically the middle of the night before I sold to the last person.

"Good work again today, Boxxo."

A familiar voice echoes behind me. Lammis, a smile on her face, comes up and stands next to me.

Normally, I would be surprised—what had she come out so late at night for? But there's a reason I'm fine with it. She's been there all along. The whole day, right nearby.

She still left when someone asked something of her, but aside from that, she never went farther than fifteen feet from me. Right now, she's wrapped in a sleeping bag, with only her head poking out. Her smile is so wide, it looks like someone put two big, curved pieces of fish together on her face.

My kidnapping must have really gotten to her. She seems to have decided she'll sleep outdoors tonight so she doesn't have to leave me alone. Hulemy and Munami tried to persuade her otherwise, but she remained stubborn and unyielding.

Director Bear seemed worried, too. He put up a guard at the Hunters Association entrance—which didn't normally have a guard—just to keep watch for us.

"I'm sure you're really tired as well, Boxxo. You have to sleep, too."

"Welcome."

Let's call it quits for today and turn out the lights.

She probably won't leave my side for a while, but there's no other vending machine out there being worried over so excessively. I'll stick with her until she decides otherwise.

"Can I talk to you until I fall asleep?"

Of course. I can't do anything but listen, but I'll listen as much as you want.

As she goes on about this and that, her voice happy, I shift my gaze to the night sky spread out overhead. It may seem like we're outdoors, but this is a dungeon, and there are no stars up there. Even though there's a sun.

My Japanese common sense doesn't apply to this fantastical dungeon scenery, and as I gaze at it, I start to really feel as though I've returned home.

Without knowing any of that, Lammis continues to talk, her full smile never leaving her face, her words carried up and away on the night's breeze.

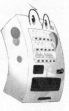

My vision rocks up and down, left and right. And sometimes, the scenery blurs swiftly by.

"Boxxo, it'll be noon soon, so let's take a break."

Lammis is helping with the reconstruction today with as much vigor as always. I can hear her voice from very close. I'm on her back, so that makes sense. I'd be fine if she let me down, though.

She's been with me constantly, ever since we returned from the kidnapping incident. Before now, she'd been setting me on the ground while she worked, but now I'm on her back no matter what. The only times she leaves are when she needs to go to the bathroom; we spend the vast majority of the day together.

I'm not unhappy with it, but...maybe she's getting a little too dependent on me.

"You two get along so well it's almost creepy. Yo, Boxxo. You doing okay?"

Hulemy waves at us and approaches, wearing her usual black garments. As always, she seems oblivious to cohesive outfits and fashion, and her frizzy hair is messily tied back.

She's put even less effort into her appearance than when she was locked up in the basement. What's going on?

"Oh, Hulemy. Are you okay now? You're not still tired, are you?"

"I'm great. When I was locked up, I ate better than I normally do, so I'm fit as a fiddle."

They seem to be very good friends. They always try to meet during break time every day.

Hulemy generally gives off the impression of an intellectual older sister, so it's funny when Lammis sometimes worries about her like her mother.

"Anyway, why not put Boxxo down while you work? Isn't he getting in the way?"

"No, not at all! I have so much strength that if I don't wear something as heavy as Boxxo, it's actually more difficult to move."

Hmm. That's not the only reason, I'm sure. I'm happy she's concerned for me, but her overprotectiveness has been excessive. Maybe we should do something about it.

"But, Lammis, if you're always there, won't it scare away his customers?"

"Ah, ngh... But if I leave, he might get kidnapped again."

"Boxxo is being more careful now, too. Right?"

"Welcome."

"W-well... If you say so, Boxxo."

Reluctantly, Lammis sets me on the ground and puffs out her cheek a little in a mild display of dissatisfaction. Now I can have some time to myself. Good job, Hulemy.

To be honest, being carried all the time has caused my sales to plummet. Only so many people are brave enough to buy something from a vending machine moving around so vigorously on someone's back. The two gatekeepers, however, called out to Lammis and got her to stop moving before they bought anything.

Lammis doesn't seem like she's focused on her work. She keeps glancing over here. I hope she doesn't get hurt.

I'm doing well for myself, though. The customers who have been waiting and watching until now are crowding in front of me. Great—now to make up for lost time.

I sold more than I expected to during the day. As I sit in front of the Hunters Association at my regular spot and refill the products that sold well, I feel so pleased with myself that all my products could have gotten warm even if they were meant to be served cold.

In the evenings, Lammis usually stays close by and eats something she purchased from me, but tonight, Hulemy had the good sense to bring her to the cafeteria that Munami and the mistress are running out of a temporary storefront.

People usually stop coming around this time, so for once, I spend some time alone with my machine self. While I am, however, someone comes walking by, head hanging slightly.

It's the young merchant, one of the three regulars I get in the mornings. Normally, he has an excessively pleasant smile and a friendly attitude, which also leaves a good impression on the other two regulars, the old couple. But now, he looks so depressed I can almost see a dark aura surrounding him.

He sighs. "It's just not working," he says to himself. "She seems busier lately than usual, and I don't even have a chance to say hello... And tomorrow's her birthday."

I put two and two together. He's fallen for Munami, the inn's poster girl, hasn't he? He wants to pursue a relationship, but he's worried because it's not going well. I'd gladly take him up on a conversation about love troubles, but I'm stuck with simple yes/no responses.

Another sigh. "I'm worried about Acowi. She's been working too hard lately."

From the exact opposite direction as the young merchant comes the giant shadow of a goril— No, it's Gocguy, assistant to the money changer. Despite how he looks, he's a calm person, the sort who would see a child who tripped and was crying, wait for them to get up on their own, and then smile and tell them what a good job they did.

"Oh, hello. Gocguy, the money changer."

"Well, this is a surprise. Thank you again for the other day."

They greet each other; they seem to be acquainted. I suppose it's not strange a merchant and a money changer would know each other. They talk about the weather, business, inoffensive topics, and the latest gossip, but their hearts don't seem into it. It's like I'm watching a bad play.

Sometimes, both of them will glance at me. They must both want to buy something. It doesn't matter if someone else is here—they can buy whatever they like. Is something wrong?

"Welcome."

"Oh," says the merchant with a start. "Would you like something to drink? My treat."

"No, no, I have a debt to Mr. Boxxo, so allow me."

They begin going back and forth with their offers. In a normal conversation, this would be the perfect chance for one to agree and get out of paying for himself.

"How about I pay this time, and when we meet again, you can treat me?" suggests the merchant.

"That sounds good," says Gocguy. "Thank you."

The young merchant drinks his usual milk tea, and Gocguy, a can of lemon tea. They both chose the warm version. It's apparently the beginning of winter, which is the perfect season for some good, hot beverages. At this point, there's no reason to question how there are seasons here even though we're inside a dungeon.

The merchant exhales. "This really calms me down."

"Mr. Boxxo has so many delicious things that it's always hard to choose."

All they're doing is having a hot drink together, but I feel like they've gotten a little closer. Their words seem more animated now.

"By the way...," begins Gocguy. "Pardon me for asking, but your face looked quite grave earlier."

"Oh, how embarrassing. I was, well, worrying over lady troubles."

"I see. Would you like to talk to me about it? Saying your worries aloud will help. Let's see. I was worried about my boss, Miss Acowi, as well. I would be thankful if you would hear me out afterward."

By adding a condition that he'd reveal his own worries, Gocguy created a situation in which the merchant could speak more freely. Acowi seemed tightly strung, not the type that would be very skilled with negotiations. He must be supporting her in that respect.

"Well, I have feelings for a certain someone, but they're unrequited. I've received information that her birthday is soon, but I'm not sure what to do. I could give her a present, but I don't know if she'd be happy to get something from one of her customers that she's not very close to."

"I see— That is a worrisome problem. Gifts are not always better the more expensive they are. If you were close to her, you could go with a jewel or an ornament, but getting such a thing from a regular customer could pique her curiosity in the wrong way."

"I thought the same. Loathe though I am to admit it, I don't have much experience in matters of the heart; it's always business for me. I don't know what would be best in this kind of situation."

He does seem like a very earnest, hardworking man. His lifestyle must not have involved anything in the way of love affairs.

If she were the type of fickle woman you might have seen in a clichéd story or video game, you could give her something expensive, and she would initially refuse it but ultimately accept it, and then her affection levels would skyrocket. Munami seems used to such people, though. She would accept it right away and that would be it.

"In this case, I believe it would be better to get her a more typical gift that any woman would be happy to receive."

"You think so, too? That was why I came here. Have you heard the rumor that Boxxo will listen to your wishes and stock new products based on that?"

"Oh, yes, I have heard that. Apparently, he doesn't only change his products but his entire shape… Between you and me, he provided the contraceptive-like items they use for Ms. Shirley's night business as well."

Word of that has gotten around, huh? It could become an urban legend—or a settlement legend—soon. Of course, maybe I already am one, being a vending machine with a mind of its own.

"We'll never know unless we try," says Gocguy. "Why not ask Mr. Boxxo? I'm interested in this as well."

"All right. We have nothing to lose. Boxxo, were you listening to all that?"

"Welcome."

"That makes things quick. Do you have anything I could give to a woman on her birthday?"

I've been mulling it over for the entire conversation, and I do have one idea.

It's good that the settlement is active, since they're in the middle of rebuilding, but it kind of seems like they have no time for anything else. They don't want for any necessary goods or materials, but sources of entertainment are sparse. I can't help but feel they have their hands full simply living their day-to-day lives.

This might be the ideal environment for hunters and merchants, but I can't call the settlement a kind place for women, even as flattery. Which means the new product I will provide them is…

"He lit up… What? He completely changed again. Are these flowers?"

"Well, isn't that an impressive array of flowers. There is a lot of wet-land in this stratum. I've never seen flowers this beautiful before."

Yes—a flower vending machine. It changes most of me to a glass pane separated into parts, with flowers lined up inside. I can only stock things I have experience buying, so I have carnations and roses I bought for Mother's Day, bouquets of flowers for grave visits, and lilies. My mother was initially going to buy them, but she ended up letting me pay. That certainly worked out in my favor.

With the settlement in the midst of restoration, building materials and rubble are strewn all over town. I don't have a single recollection of any flowers. In a place like this, most women would be happy to receive a colorful bouquet. At least, I think so.

"I see—flowers. The prices are reasonable, too. This is good!"

"If I recall correctly, Ms. Acowi likes white flowers. I'll buy some as well."

The pair purchases the flowers that they each want. The merchant purchased an assortment of flowers that you would typically find at a Japanese graveside or a household altar. Gocguy purchased the white lilies.

Mine can't be the only heart warmed by seeing two men holding bouquets like this.

They look at the flowers in their hands, faces softening as they blush a little, then say their good-byes and walk away. I hope things go well for them both. I'll have to pay extra-close attention to any information that comes my way.

"Boxxo, have you heard?"

Several days passed after that. We're apparently on the precipice of the real winter, and the residents are hurriedly making preparations to last through the cold season. While I'm doing my expected business in my usual spot, Lammis suddenly comes at me with a question.

There's no way for me to know what she's talking about, so I answer with a "Too bad."

"Well, you know how Munami and the mistress made a makeshift cafeteria in a tent? It's really, really popular with girls right now. Why do you think that is?"

I don't know. I barely have any information, so how should I respond? Cafeterias normally profit from tasty food. But if it's been popular with women, that gets me thinking. A pair of women are the ones managing it, and I've heard before that female hunters and residents find it easier to visit.

Does that mean they arranged something that appealed to an even higher demand of women? I don't know.

"Too bad."

"I didn't think you would. Actually! Munami started decorating the cafeteria with flowers. Really pretty ones, too. Just looking at them is soothing!"

Oh! It looks like the young merchant's frequent visits and purchases since then have paid off. Come to think of it, the money changer Acowi came the other day, and her face looked a little less stern. Looks like they got instant results.

I wonder if Lammis likes flowers. I could see her eyes sparkling as she talked about them.

Well then, there's only one thing to do. Yep.

"Whoa, wh-what's wrong? You suddenly changed shape... Wait, Boxxo, you were the one selling those flowers?"

After transforming into flower-vending mode, I drop a pink carnation into my compartment.

"Huh? You're giving me one, too?! Thanks, Boxxo. I'll treasure it!"

She hugs the flower and twirls around joyfully. It's the kind of happy response that makes a gift worth giving.

Did you know this, Lammis? In the language of flowers, pink carnations can mean *gratitude*.

Hulemy's Magic Tools

"Well, have a seat... Wait, you can't. Whoops, my bad."

I've returned to the settlement, the customers have started to calm down, and I'm back to my ordinary daily life. Or so I thought, right before Hulemy kidnapped me.

Actually, it would be more accurate to say that I was brought against my will into a tent she's been squatting in. By Lammis.

The sun has set below the horizon, and 80 percent of the settlement's residents are asleep at this hour.

The culprit who carried me here is sitting in bed, hugging a cushion, swaying unsteadily. She must be ready to pass out, herself.

"There's only one reason I called you here. I wanted to do some investigating. First off, you can't have a conversation unless someone knows you well, right? I'll only be asking yes-or-no questions, so they'll be easy. You can consider this overtime from when we were captive."

So that's how it is. I'm genuinely pleased she's trying to learn more about me.

Bring it on. Ask me anything you want. I'll answer everything I can—

—is how I feel initially, but then she comes at me with several questions I can't help but think aren't really that important.

"Can you feel pain? Do you have senses like humans?"

I get where she's coming from with those sorts of questions, but as things dragged on to the second half, they started getting weird.

"Do you have a lover?"

Is that present tense, or is she referring to my past life? If she means now, then of course I don't. I'm a vending machine.

Still, someone who chased only vending machines in his life, and was constantly broke because of it, would never have a girlfriend. Just give her an answer... Either one is fine, really...

"Too bad."

"Hmm. You don't, huh?"

Why is she smiling? Why does she look happy? Does she feel like her strong-minded personality keeps men away despite her physical beauty, and now she's found a friend? Maybe she thinks I'm a comrade in misery.

"Then, I have to ask. You're good friends with Lammis, so, well... Do you, uh, like her?"

She helps me out all the time, so if I had to say one way or another, then of course I do. She's a nice person, and without her, I wouldn't even be able to move.

"Welcome."

"Huh, I see. Makes sense. She's bright and fun to be around. She might be a little clumsy, but men think that kind of thing is cute, right?"

She's complimenting her childhood friend, but for some reason she looks a little unhappy.

"Hey, and this isn't really related, but I figured I'd ask, just to get your opinion. Your soul is male, right?"

"Welcome." I may look like a vending machine, but I'm still a man inside. Probably.

"So, ah, again, this is just so I know, and there's no downside to having as much information as possible. That's my motto, after all. Well... Boxxo, do I seem like a charming person to you?"

I understand the importance of having information. Why is she talking so fast? She's asking a vending machine—is she still embarrassed anyway?

Hulemy is a little obstinate and bullheaded, but she gives the impression of an older sister always looking out for her younger siblings. And at her core, she's a kind, beautiful person. My answer is obvious.

"Welcome."

"O-oh, I see. I'm grateful for that, even if it was flattery. Thanks, Boxxo."

She scratches at her nose with a finger, her cheeks reddening in a blush. It's unimaginably cuter than her normal face. I think my machinery might start groaning in a second. She'd be more popular with guys if she made faces like that more often.

"Ack, that question wasn't like me at all. I'm a little bad when it comes to that stuff. I just figured you'd listen and not make fun of me—that's all. Sorry."

There's no need to apologize. I don't have very many good memories involving women, but if you have any worries or anything you want to discuss with me, I'll hear you out. Of course, I can't exactly give my own opinion.

"All right. Back to the subject."

Hulemy goes back to her old self after that, inquiring after every little detail about me, like what I can do and what happens to the money. I'll add that in the meantime, Lammis has long since drifted off into a dream world during our conversation.

Hulemy began buying things from me every day after that.

One day, she comes to me like she always does but asks me not to make the bottle disappear after she's done drinking from it. She seems to want to research the plastic bottle's materials.

I don't have any reason to refuse, so I agree, and she grins happily, saying "I'll make something you'll find useful as thanks," and leaves.

Come to think of it, Hulemy is a famous magic-item engineer, isn't she? According to Lammis, she's invented a lot, and makes quite a bit from it. I know firsthand how insightful and smart she is, so when I hear her say that, I can easily accept it. She's going to develop a magic item for me as thanks, is she? I look forward to it.

A few days later, Hulemy walks to me with such a light step I almost expect her to start skipping.

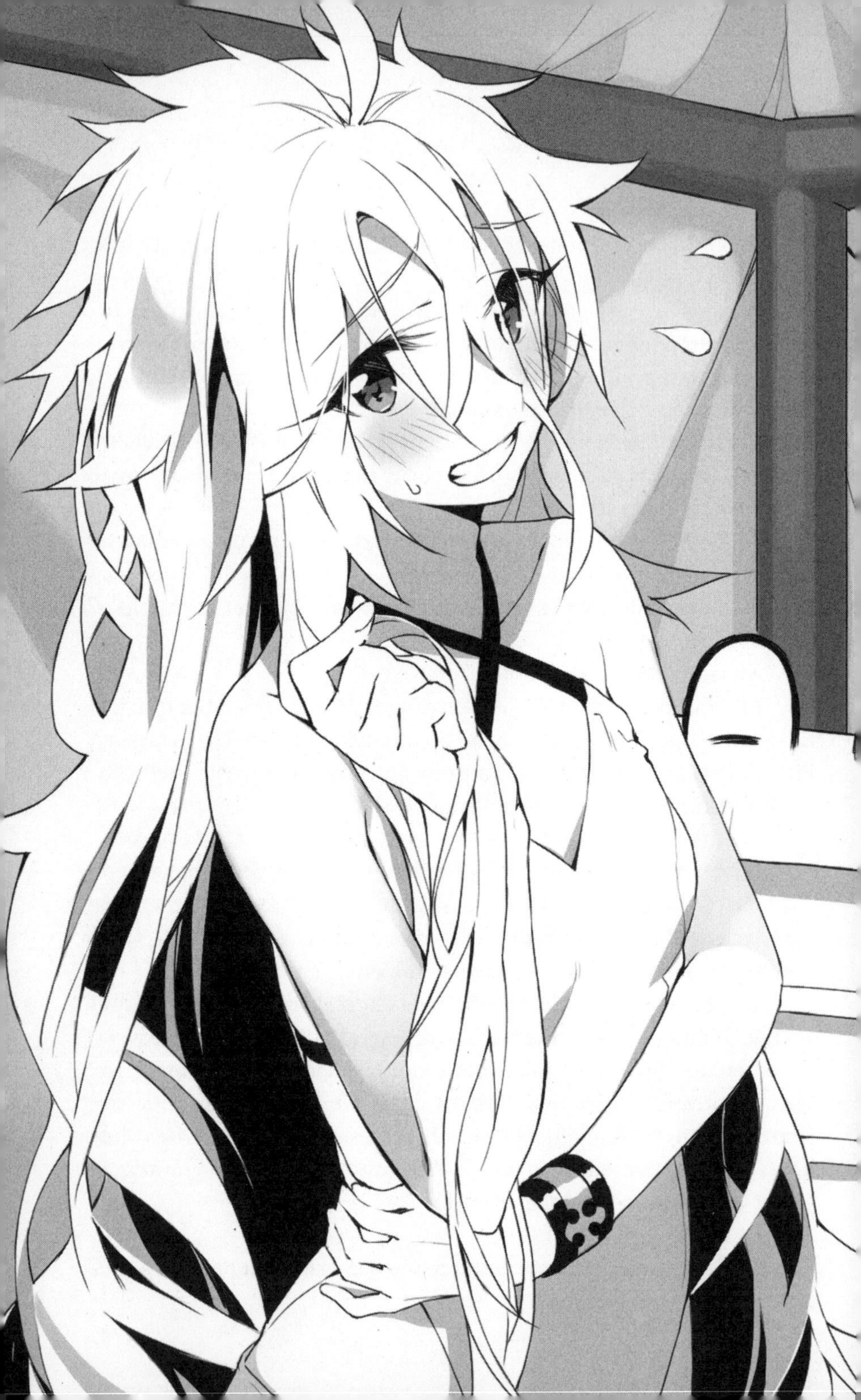

"Boxxo, I brought what I promised."

That's a dubious way of putting it, but she must be talking about the magic item she mentioned.

She holds it out. It closely resembles the portable, egg-shaped game that was a fad some time ago. It's a handy size, small enough to hide in your palm.

What could it be? It has what looks like a little screen on it, which is solidifying the handheld video-game image for me even more.

"This magic item has a translation function for your soul. Considering you say you're a soul inside a magic item, but you can't talk, I decided I should just go through your soul and ask your mind directly. That's what I developed it for."

That's amazing—if it's true. But even in this world, filled with mysterious and incomprehensible powers like magic and Blessings, that can't be possible. Maybe it would be if it were a Blessing, but I don't think you can do something like that with a tool.

"Heh, Boxxo, you're dubious, aren't you?"

"Welcome."

"How honest of you. Well, I don't hate that kind of thing. I'll explain, then. There's a certain monster with the Blessing to read someone's thoughts. It's infamous as a tricky monster to beat, but rarely, it will drop a dark-red gemstone. Basically, I embedded one of those gems in a tool, then drew a magic circle on the inside to amplify its mana. And you can't just draw any old thing. Its size, pattern, and even its coloration are all related. Anyway, that's entirely a secret, but there's a lot of magic-item engineers who would try to steal that stuff. They don't write down rules and technology for it, so I've got everything hammered into my head."

Whenever Hulemy talks about magic items, her expression gets livelier. She does it when she's researching me, too. She must really like this sort of thing. You do much better work when you love what you do, after all.

"Sorry, I'm off topic again. Whenever I talk about my technical knowledge, I start rambling on and on. Anyway, what I'm trying to say is that with this thing, I can listen to what your mind is saying. It's still a prototype, so this will just be a test run."

If this is true, then it's an unheard-of invention. Sh-she can hear my mind's voice... If I think anything strange, she might start to think I'm a pervert. Clear your mind. Clear your mind... Wait, if I do that, will she be able to hear anything at all?

"So can I try it out? I mean, I might hear something you don't want other people to know, so..."

H-hmm. I'm a bit scared, but it's more important that I have a chance to communicate with her. My worldly passions have waned ever since becoming a vending machine, so it should be fine.

"Welcome."

"Oh, you're okay with it? Thanks a bunch! Let's get right to the testing. The way it works is, when I press this button, I'll be able to hear nearby souls speaking through this magic item. I'm pressing it now."

She seems nervous, too, but I'm so nervous my body might freeze solid. Though I guess I'm already a solid object.

Hulemy's slender finger presses the switch. If I think something now, will it turn into words? Actually, would these words I'm thinking now replay for her?

"Ahh, I want her."

I hear a more mechanical, synthetic voice than mine from the magic item.

Huh? N-no, I wasn't thinking anything like that!

Hulemy looks at me, eyes narrowed. N-no! I wasn't thinking that. How could a vending machine *want* her like that?!

"Boxxo, you're more vulgar than I thought."

"Too bad. Too bad." Wait, repeating *too bad* makes it sound like I'm talking about myself!

"What are you doing, Boxxo? Oh, Hulemy's here, too, eh?"

Karios walks up, his hair cleanly shaven, his shining bald head his trademark.

"Hey, it's Karios, the gatekeeper. You headed to work?"

"Yeah. Gorth decided not to wake me up today and went up by himself, the bastard. I'm headed to the gate now. Boxxo, can I get the usual? I'd like that revitalizing water today."

Revitalizing water—he must mean the sports drink. And his usual set is the pressed potato chips plus a can of oden.

"Thank you."

"No problem. All right, I've got to hurry over now."

Just as Karios raises a hand to say good-bye and turns around to head to the gate, the magic item responds again.

"Such a pretty face. Shame about her breasts and personality. Talk about a waste."

Hulemy's look is getting much more dangerous.

No, no, it wasn't me! I didn't think that just now! And actually, that just *had* to be Karios's mind! Which is how I want to plead my case to clear up this misunderstanding, but I can't talk!

Hulemy, who has gotten this completely wrong, steadily glares at me through narrowed eyes. Crap. I have to do something to tell her that Karios is the culprit.

I drop a can of juice into my compartment, then use Force Field to launch it toward him.

It doesn't end up hitting him, but it rolls to a stop in front of him. He notices it, picks it up, and then brings it back to me. "Hey, Boxxo. This came flying out. I'll just leave it here."

"Thank you."

Hopefully, now Hulemy will realize those words came from his mind.

"She's got a nice butt, though."

"Huh?" mutters Karios, responding to the voice he heard from the magic item.

Hulemy's gaze turns, with slow, twitching motions, to Karios, piercing him with her laser-like glare.

"I, you, what?!" cries Karios, completely bewildered, a bead of sweat trickling down his brow.

"Ah, I see. Karios thinks my breasts and personality are no good, now, does he? Heh. I see how it is."

She's…scaring me. Beneath her low, intimidating voice and narrowed eyes is a smile, but her eyes are cold and menacing.

"H-how did you know what I was think— Ack!"

Oh, now you've done it, Karios. You just admitted to it.

He's still confused, but he likely senses a threat to his well-being. He pounds a fist into his hand, says "Oh, right, my job" as though he's just remembered, then runs away like a fleeing hare.

"Bastard… Sorry, Boxxo. I misunderstood. I apologize."

"Welcome."

I'm saved. Somehow. But when I think about it calmly, that magic item is incredible. For some reason, it couldn't pick up my mind's voice, but it definitely transmitted every bit of Karios's inner thoughts.

"I can't hear you from this, Boxxo, but technically it worked, since it heard his mind. It has room for improvement."

I'm both excited and terrified to have her finish this. If she can hear people's thoughts with it, disasters similar to Karios's slipup may occur.

"Anyway, I'll fiddle with it some more, and—"

"So it wasn't Boxxo who said I had a nice butt, huh? Hmm. Damn."

Hmm? Wait, was that voice I just heard from the magic item…?

"Heh, I…I…I see— *Uwaaahhhh!*"

Hulemy's face goes beet-red as she slams the magic item into the ground and starts stomping it to little pieces before I have a chance to stop her.

Um, Hulemy?

"Allll righty, then! Looks like it doesn't work after all. I'll have to redo the whole thing. Ah-ha-ha-ha-ha-ha. See ya!"

She spins around, but not before I catch a glimpse of her bright-red face in profile. Then she runs off just as fast as Karios did.

This day has been full of ups and downs, but I got one good thing out of it: getting to see a few different sides of Hulemy that I hadn't expected. At least, that's how I've decided to look at it.

Incidentally, Hulemy did try to remake the device once more after that, but she never did complete a mind-reading magic item.

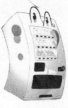

Marvels

There are four wall-mounted candlesticks in the room.

A large, round table lies in the dimly lit room's center, and thirteen figures sit around it.

Silence envelops the room. No one opens their mouth—until one woman rises abruptly.

"Thank you all for coming. Let's begin our regular meeting. I'm sure everyone knows the agenda for today."

The suspicious words cause a stir among the others at the table.

"I never believed they'd get this far."

"Indeed. We let our guard down."

"Without a plan, they will wipe us out in the blink of an eye."

Words of concern left the attendees' mouths one after the other, their voices strained and sorrowful.

The low illumination on their faces revealed dark, lifeless masks.

"Order. I've summarized the information we have thus far... If you would."

Seated next to the speaker, a woman in clothing resembling a maid's outfit rises at the request and opens the folder of documents in front of her. "They have seventy percent of the opened dungeon stratums under their control. Now, they've reached us. We must spare no effort to come together as a unified group and eliminate them. For that purpose,

I've invited someone who is to be our trump card. A few words, if you please."

"Welcome."

That's the only thing I can say, having been forced into a meeting between those authoritative eateries in the Clearflow Lake stratum's settlement.

This meeting is held three times a year on the same days, and sometimes they have serious discussions, but they generally just trade information and end it with idle chatter.

This one, however, was announced in a hurry as an exception, and no one appears relaxed. They look like cornered rats, and that honestly makes me uncomfortable.

"If you have any opinion on the matter, Mr. Boxxo, you may speak at your discretion."

It creeps me out when Munami adds "Mr." to my name. So she's the type to completely immerse herself in a given role, is she? She's the spitting image of a talented secretary.

"Allow me to continue. Currently, a large number of people are moving into this settlement. Our population has increased by approximately one hundred, and there are rumors that our residence now numbers close to five hundred."

"Well, it has been a lot livelier lately."

"Normally, that would be cause for celebration."

No matter how many hands they have for the settlement's reconstruction, it won't be enough, so people have been coming and going rapidly as we try to, at the very least, get the outer wall repaired for the winter. We've managed to procure just enough logs to get the job done, which has apparently set everyone's minds at ease.

"It would normally be a very joyous occasion for the food industry to have more potential customers…but the sudden increase in people has also led to *them* making a move. You know them—their goal is to control all food in the dungeon. The ultimate evil in eateries—the Chains Restaurant!"

"Damn. Without them here, I thought I would be able to make some money!"

"I was doing business on another stratum when those buar-headed merchants stole that settlement's whole food demand!"

As I watch the eatery owners act like the protagonists of a tragedy, I summarize it in my mind.

Each stratum in this dungeon has a settlement where people gather, and this massive restaurant business has a location in each settlement. In other words, a true labyrinth "chain" restaurant.

With the population at around only a hundred before now, they hadn't bothered with us, since they didn't think we'd be very profitable. With the recent uptick in people, however, they must have decided now was a good time to come.

This big chain's name seems to be a reference to literal chains. Their locations are so big, you wouldn't think they were eating establishments. Not only do they have food and drink, they also have a wide variety of preserved foodstuffs and take-home ingredients to support their catchphrase: *The Chains Restaurant, for all your food needs.*

They have connections with the workers of the transfer circle as well, and they can use it at a discount, so they don't incur transportation costs for foods. That leads to a pricing and quality normal eateries can't match.

And for any settlement the Chains Restaurant moves into, there's really only one outcome the local food industry can expect: total defeat.

This stuff happens a lot in modern Japan, too. There are plenty of examples of big stores built in an area that crush smaller shops and dominate entire streets, leading to rows and rows of shuttered-up stalls.

"They must have been waiting for a time like this. Winter rolls in, and we've been trading for food at high prices—and with how cheaply they sell theirs, there won't be any reason to worry. They possess many magic items that make it possible to keep food fresh, so they'll be able to provide the same meals even in the wintertime."

I wonder if those tools are like big refrigerators. Eighty percent of the eateries here are open-air, so they obviously wouldn't have anything like that. They can't stock ingredients, so they would have closed up today.

"They have their fingers in the transfer circle business, too. They're blatantly starting to drive up prices, which is strangling the circulation of food. We're trapped like rats at the moment."

"Damn it all! Is waiting for them to trample us all we can do?"

"I have two adorable children at home. How are we supposed to last the winter?!"

Fists pound on the table. The store owners are visibly frustrated by all this. It's especially clear from how they keep glancing over in my direction.

This extended farce has allowed me figure out the reason they called me here. They expect me to come up with a way to turn this situation around.

To be honest, as a vending machine, it doesn't really matter to me if a big chain moves into town. I can operate twenty-four hours a day, and I have several products the Chains Restaurant can't imitate. I don't think the residents of this world could use the freeze-dry manufacturing method for cup ramen, for instance.

But I like the people living here, and I have Lammis to think about, too. It's of no cost to me to show them favor. I'd like to secure a home for when I break down one day and become unusable.

I also have a bitter memory of a favorite shop of mine in my school days, run by an old couple, that was squashed by big business. It wouldn't be so bad to have my revenge in this world.

"So, Mr. Boxxo, will you cooperate with us?! ...If you do, we'll halve Lammis's inn fees when we finish rebuilding it."

Munami leans in close as she whispers the Lammis part to me; if I had a physical body, I'm sure I would have reacted. Hmm... I planned to help out even without her negotiations, but if this will benefit Lammis, any reason I might have to refuse has been eliminated.

"Welcome."

"Thank you so much, Mr. Boxxo!"

"Ohhh! If Boxxo helps us, we'll have the strength of one hundred men...one hundred boxes!"

"With Boxxo, we might just be able to pull through!"

I'm fine with them making a big deal out of it, but this is all going to be my responsibility, isn't it? They're excited, thinking they've already won. What would they do if I can't help them at all?

I want to heave a sigh, but it would only produce a canned phrase, so I endure.

"So this is the Chains Restaurant, huh? I've heard the rumors, but wow, it's big!"

"Looks like this place has finally made it to our stratum, eh?"

I've come with Lammis and Hulemy to spy on the enemy. We're in front of the store now. It's definitely not the size of a shopping mall, but it's probably the second largest building I've seen in this world, next to the Hunters Association building.

The ceiling is domed, and it looks like it has one story. A circular store made of warped wooden panels fitted into one another. The design stands out prominently in the settlement.

The entrance is large, and in front of it are employees in almost-pure-yellow jackets calling out to attract customers.

"Welcome, welcome. Welcome to the Chains Restaurant, your friendly neighborhood store with delicious foods at low prices! Chains Restaurant, at your service! And as a store-opening celebration, all products are half price—that's right, folks, half price!"

I'm starting to feel nostalgic. You see this kind of thing all the time in Japan, but it seems like a foreign element in this world. An endless stream of people step inside, attracted by how unusual it is.

They're flourishing. Are their name and accolades lending to their success? I can understand those new to this settlement wanting to choose this store over the smaller shops.

"Oh, oh my. Well, well, well. Come to scout out the enemy, perhaps?"

A slender man calling for customers walks over to us, rubbing his hands together. The businesslike smile on his face gives me the creeps.

"H-how did you know what we were doing?"

"Lammis... Behind you," says Hulemy, putting a hand to her forehead, shaking it tiredly.

I mean, I think anyone would figure it out if you're carrying me on your back. Does she not realize how much we stand out?

"That must be Boxxo, the magic item with a mind I've heard so much about. Our president is interested in you, too. Are you interested in working for us? I can guarantee that you will be treated well."

I didn't expect a recruitment offer. He doesn't seem like he's joking. His eyes aren't smiling.

From the other side's perspective, I'm the biggest obstacle here. Is their intention to rope me into their business instead?

"Boxxo won't work in a place like that. He'll be with me forever. Right, Boxxo?"

"Welcome."

"See?"

Why is Lammis sticking out her chest and acting smug? Still, now that I've been reincarnated in another world, I've frankly no interest in a normal, stable workplace. If I worked here, I have a feeling it would be no different from being a supermarket vending machine.

"That is unfortunate. Well, I'm sure you'll come around in a few months. Now then, we are quite busy, so I will take my leave."

What are you talking about? You were the one who came to us.

I thought Lammis and Hulemy, their enthusiasm spoiled, would turn around and leave. But we can't go back without doing anything, so they enter the store with me behind them.

The entrance is large enough for them to go through it with a vending machine, and inside the store, there are no partition walls, creating a big, wide-open space. To the right is where they sell food. It looks like they offer dried beef and other ingredients that will last a long time. The goods seem aimed mainly at hunters.

Left of the center is a wide counter with a kitchen behind it—probably the kind where you order and it's prepared for you to take on the spot. Long tables are set up as well, with chairs spaced at even intervals. It has a similar setup to a food court.

Lammis orders meat and pasta with yellowish-green vegetables in it. Hulemy asks for bread and something that looks like a whitefish meunière. They both look delicious to me, but they're really no different from the ordinary stuff you can get in any old cafeteria.

"Hmm, it's good in a normal way," says Lammis.

"Yeah," agrees Hulemy. "It tastes just like you think it would."

As they eat their food, they don't really show any emotion. I don't have taste buds. Not being able to compare foods stings, but it must taste good. I don't see any of the joy of eating coming from them, though. They both seem happy whenever they eat my stuff.

"It's good, but… It's just kind of normal."

"Maybe we're too used to Boxxo's food. I'm not surprised or impressed. It's good in a normal way."

I see. It's the kind of flavor you tend to get at above-average Chains Restaurants. They don't use any strong seasonings so everyone will like it. Rather than going for a hundred points, they aim to keep it above seventy. Not that there's anything wrong with that—every shop has to have a unified sense of taste. They can't use complex recipes and spices. Plus, the prices here are the selling point, so they can only spend so much on ingredients.

To add to that, spices are valuable in this world, meaning saltiness and light flavors are commonplace.

Maybe there's something we can exploit in that.

The menu seems to be sticking to the basics as well. Yes, yes—I think I'm starting to get an idea.

Overthrow the Chains Restaurant!

"We will now begin our second grand gathering to overthrow the Chains Restaurant!"

"*Yeeeaaahhh!*"

The female shopkeepers, unable to match the impassioned roars of the men, shyly raised fists in the air in support; a scene that was unintentionally cute.

It looks like we have the same members as before. I guess they've settled on Munami as moderator.

We're currently inside the tent the inn mistress is operating temporarily. The table and chairs are mostly pressed up against one wall, creating a fair amount of open space.

"As we notified you all beforehand, today we'll be discussing countermeasures; namely, the cultivation of new recipes. I hope you've come with new samples. We'll start things off."

They begin arranging new recipe prototypes around the table. The shopkeepers sample them and share opinions. Eventually, they each finish submitting their own dishes, but to be honest, none of them quite hits the nail on the head.

They're all slight variations on preexisting recipes. I don't know how they taste, but judging from the others' reactions, the situation looks grim.

"Now we turn to you, Mr. Boxxo. Thank you for attending once again. Might you have any advice? What do you think of my test recipe, for example?"

Munami holds a plate out in front of me—pasta with a thick soup on it. It looks like pasta with a béchamel sauce, but instead of being white, it's yellow.

"Um, Boxxo, you seem a bit troubled. How about Hulemy and I eat it and give you our thoughts?"

"Welcome."

Ah, right. Lammis and Hulemy are attending the meeting today as honorary guests. The shopkeepers must want to get opinions from a customer's perspective as well.

I'd be happy to let you guys taste them in my stead.

"Boxxo says it's okay. Munami, can we try it?"

"Yes, of course, Lammis. Go right ahead. You too, Hulemy."

"Not sure I have a very sophisticated palate, but all right."

They bring the pasta with yellow soup to their mouths. They chew it over in silence, then wipe their mouths.

"It tastes good to me," says Lammis. "But maybe it's a little bland? I think it might be because the soup uses animal broth, but you thickened it with vegetables. I think the pasta would taste better if it was a little richer."

"Yeah, that's what it feels like. And maybe you could cook the pasta a little less, so it's harder. If it has time to soak in the soup, it should be easier to eat."

Those were pretty exact opinions. Lammis is apparently decent at cooking for herself, and it looks like Hulemy's boasting that her food rivals first-class chefs' was no lie. Maybe she has a more refined palate since she's eaten that kind of food from a young age.

"H-hold on a moment. I'll write that down. Um, Boxxo, what about you?"

Munami, flustered, has dropped the theatrics and speaks normally. She wants my opinion? I did think of something other than the improvements they suggested. Let's see—if you want thick, creamy pasta, then how about this pasta with white sauce?

I have canned soup with pasta here as well, but for them, the point is that the pasta will soak in the soup for a while, so they don't use normal pasta. Using that as a reference might be a little strange.

Instead, I bring out pasta sold in a specialty vending machine I found on a ferry once. The soup and the pasta are separate, and it takes longer to cut the plastic sealing on it than it does to open a regular can, but I remember it tasting particularly good.

"*Fwah*, is this pasta in a bag? Hmm. This is warm, but you have to cut the seal away, right? It has a picture of scissors drawn on it, so you cut here and pour it inside... It's white. A mixture of mushrooms and smoked meat, hmm? Let's see how it tastes... Mmm, this is good! It has a rich flavor, and the soup is thick, too. It's made with milk, isn't it? Yes, yes, in that case..."

Munami grabs her notes and heads for the kitchen, evidently having learned something.

When the shopkeepers see her go, they immediately swarm around me, and Lammis and Hulemy end up sampling one test recipe after another.

Karaage and french fries for those running fried-food stands.

Pork soup, *shijimi* clam soup, and plain miso soup for the shop-keepers of hot soup places. Miso doesn't appear to exist here, but the shopkeepers nod to themselves, obviously drawing inspiration from it.

A pair of twin girls apparently provide the settlement with sweets, so I give them crepes in a clear container that I ate once in Kagoshima prefecture. The crepes in that vending machine were locally famous. There were many varieties, each one delicious.

The ladies loved the crepes; I think those working in the shop run by the ever-voluptuous Shirley will receive them well. I feel that if nearby shops sell them, they'll see quite a bit more business.

In the same way, I offer food that matches the other shopkeepers' respective repertoires. They get advice from Lammis and Hulemy, take their own notes, and then start working on all kinds of improvements right on the spot. Now it's time for me to do some business.

"Huh? Boxxo, you changed shape again. Are those eggs?"

Yes. This time, I changed into an egg vending machine. Egg vending machines are surprisingly popular, and you can frequently find them all over Japan.

They seem to be having a rough time getting ingredients, so the eggs fly off my shelves. After that, I shift into a vegetable vending machine commonly seen locally, causing the shopkeepers to fight over who gets to buy them first.

I make sure to sell milk as well, since it's required for the pasta sauce and the crepes. Unfortunately, I've never run across a vending machine that sold raw meat before, so I can't do anything about that. I don't think they'd have them in Japan for food hygiene reasons. We'll have to have the hunters do that work for us. I set the products at pretty attractive prices. The shopkeepers seem to be more than happy with my marketing, so they decide to set aside a bit of time once a week for me to sell them ingredients. They plead for me to do this for at least for the duration of the winter, so I accept.

Three days later, it's time for our all-out restaurant revolt.

Today, I refrain from stocking foods during the eateries' hours to support their activities. I selected a lineup of drinks that I think will go well with their new recipes.

The bout will last for one month, while the Chains Restaurant's grand opening sale is still going on. In that time, we will stop the outflow of customers and gain control over their stomachs.

The Chains Restaurant is known for withdrawing immediately if they decide they're not turning a profit, so if their grand opening sale numbers are poor, there's a good chance they'll stop doing business on the Clearflow Lake stratum.

I've done all I can, so now I just have to wait for the results. I had them position me in a place where I could see a lot of shops at once, so for today, I'll be a close observer.

In the morning, all the shops are busy preparing—but right before noon, each one springs into action.

"We've got a new recipe on the menu today, folks! Crisp, fried putetu, all the rage with kids! Come and try them out!"

"One dish, packed with all the rich flavors of meat. You can only try it here!"

"After such a rich meal, how about a light dessert that's a feast for the eyes? You can choose any fruit you like as a filling!"

The hawkers begin raising their voices, calling out for customers.

It's been two weeks since the Chains Restaurant set up shop, and the customers have just gotten a taste of their most noteworthy foods. Now, products lined the streets that they'd never seen nor heard of before.

All of it was pretty much junk food. None of the foods fit into a well-balanced diet, and they're all high in calories. Still, the people of this world burn way more calories in comparison to modern Japan.

In fact, a scarcity of vegetables in the winter is normal here; it's no use worrying about it. Anything with vegetables gets more expensive this time of year, so telling people you tried to make the food healthier by adding veggies at an extra cost would only deter customers. For stalls with hamburgers, simply adding a piece of lettuce is extravagant—and yet, burgers are lauded as inexpensive.

Each stall has been set up so as not to overlap their unique flavors, but at the moment, the *karaage* is selling the best. Second is hamburgers, and then a food that looks like *takoyaki*. They don't have octopus, so they must be using some other meat. I was the one who provided the sauce for it. Vending machines sell it normally, and I bought it several times while I was alive.

The stalls are set up in the plaza in front of the Hunters Association, giving it the added advantage of attracting hunters who've just turned in requests and filled their wallets, making them ripe for the spending. The Chains Restaurant requires a hefty plot of land to accommodate its size, so they built it somewhat far away. With the winter chill, some people were reluctant to travel that far.

Steam billows from the stalls and delicious smells waft through the air, whetting the appetites of potential customers. Who could resist such temptation? Lammis and Hulemy did the taste testing, and the shop-keepers have improved their recipes considerably, puffing them up with confidence.

"Oh? What's this?"

One hunter, who stood at a stall as he ate, was handed a business card–size slip of paper by the shopkeeper. He tilted his head in confusion.

"When you buy something, you get a stamp. Basically, once all the

spaces are stamped, you'll get a one-silver-coin discount at all participating locations."

"Really? How neat. Wait, so it doesn't have to be this shop?"

"No. It will work at any shop with this card's picture drawn on the
front."

That is the second phase of our secret plan: introducing point cards.
As for the participating locations, that refers to, of course, all the eateries
managed by the shopkeepers who were part of the council.

How did they think up the point-card system? Thanks to me, of
course. These days, vending machines that allow you to insert cards to
earn points aren't unusual. Depending on the manufacturer, some vending machines give you a point card when you buy a product, so I acquired
that feature and then actually gave them a card so they'd understand.

Well, the shopkeepers didn't know what it was for. Hulemy understood how to use it, though, and told them for me. Her powers of insight
are a huge boon.

My makeshift knowledge and Hulemy's and Lammis's advice had
roused the Clearflow Lake eateries to action, and now we find ourselves
in an advantageous position. Customers are drawn here only because of
the novelty, but that's fine for now. If we can maintain our advantage for
a short time, the Chains Restaurant should withdraw.

We had an overwhelming lead during the day, and the Chains street
advertiser's frustrated glare when he came to check things out was oh,
so satisfying.

The stalls closed up early because of the harsh night chills, but we
advertised the shops that accept the point cards today, so people still
flowed into the inn's makeshift tent and stores where their point cards
were applicable.

Unlike during the day, they're now providing soup and fried foods
with lavish amounts of vegetables at low prices. These dishes are popular with those who ate heavily earlier, as well as women and the elderly.

Of course, the only reason they can charge so little is because I set
my own prices to the bare minimum. Nevertheless, it doesn't mean I
have a net loss of points. I'm essentially keeping the eateries alive, even
though they'll go back to being my competition once the Chains Restaurant withdraws, but I don't think there's anything wrong with that.

Lammis longs for the hunt. She's focusing on rebuilding the settlement right now, but once we get through the winter, she'll probably want to start hunting work again. Stabilizing the settlement's food supply should draw in new people and allow it to prosper.

And I think she may be acting in consideration of me. The settlement has been seeking out my help more than I believe it needs to, which restricts what she can do, and I want to solve that.

Anyway, I have a lot of ideas on the matter, but in truth…I came all this way to a different world, and I want to go out and see and experience more of it.

Oh, but a customer is here. To start, I'll do my job as a vending machine.

"Welc ome."

"Yo, Boxxo. Seems like you're having a good time. Mind having a little chat? Got something to talk to you about, from one man to another—you're a man, right? Anyway, what do you say?"

One look at Captain Kerioyl's customary flippant attitude and the alarms start going off. I have a bad feeling about this.

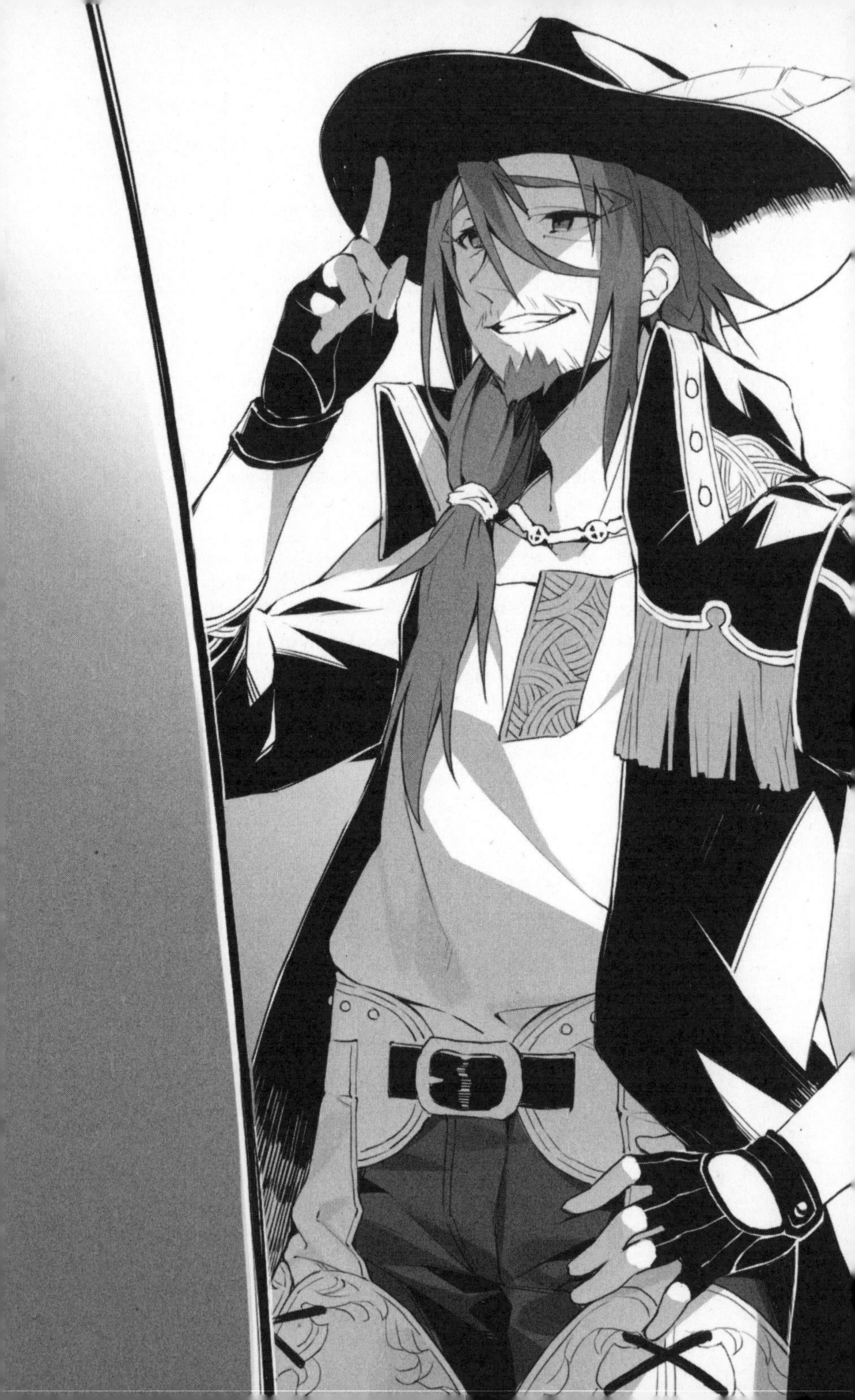

An Expedition and Diplomacy

"First, I don't mind if we wait until winter is over. Would you like to go with us on an expedition?"

I don't even give a moment's thought to Captain Kerioyl's sudden proposition. "Too bad," I answer. I figured this was what he'd ask me, so there was no reason to hesitate.

If I went, Lammis would, too, since we come as a set. I can't make a decision in this case on my own. I'll leave it to her.

"Quick with the answers as usual, eh, Boxxo? Do you not like me? Is that it?"

"Welcome."

"Seriously... You've got to treat your clients with kindness. I hate to bring this up, but we *were* the first ones to volunteer to rescue you. I'm not trying to guilt-trip you, but we didn't exactly come away unscathed. Though that doesn't mean you should feel compelled to do anything one way or another."

He's right. I do owe him a debt—a debt to the Menagerie of Fools. I'm deeply aware. I'm just uncomfortable with how shady the captain acts. I can't do more than guess, but I get the feeling he's the type who would betray you with a smile.

But he does have a point. The Menagerie of Fools aided me and easily wiped out that band of thieves.

"Welcome."

"Oh, willing to open up a bit now? Anyway, I realize I'll have to talk to Lammis, too. We still have a while before winter ends. You've got plenty of time to think it over."

Captain Kerioyl leaves. There's no point racking my brain over this. The only thing that matters is Lammis's opinion.

Er, but right now, we're overthrowing the Chains Restaurant. Night has settled in, so the shops look like they're closing up. I think every one of them got easily over three times the customers they did yesterday. Talk about roaring business. If they keep this up for the next two weeks, we might have a shot.

I shelve the captain's request for the moment. I have to focus.

After that, the ratings came piling in, customers increased by the day, and after just two weeks, we'd stolen most of them back.

For the last few days, snow has frequently fallen from early evening into night, which was a stroke of luck—the plaza in front of the Hunters Association is closer to the residential area, meaning more people have been coming to the eateries to warm themselves, too.

One month after the Chains Restaurant opened shop, they withdrew from the Clearflow Lake stratum just as easily as they'd come. I suppose it is very much like a big, popular chain to know when to pull out so cleanly, but it still makes me feel like we outsmarted them.

The shopkeepers are happy, so I guess I'm not unhappy with the result, but they left so easily that I can't help but think something else is going on. At any rate, I suppose the apprehensions of spring coming and the hunters going back to work are gone.

Ah, right—about the deal where the Menagerie of Fools invited us to come with them on an expedition in the spring. I talked it over with Lammis, and we decided to accept.

Their expedition would last two weeks in total, if that, and their mission was to scout out certain monsters and eliminate them if possible.

After talking it over and making the decision, Lammis, Hulemy, and I are all here. We couldn't let other people overhear, so I was with the two childhood friends inside the tent they were renting.

"The Menagerie of Fools is, like, seriously famous. I know we should be happy to have this chance, but… Will we be all right?"

"Hmm. The captain said if I'm afraid of fighting, I can just carry Boxxo, but I want to fight. If I don't, I'll never be able to get stronger."

As Lammis clenches her fist, her expression grows much more serious than usual. In fact, it's a little scary.

I can feel the strength of her resolve just from looking at her. Hulemy told me why she wants to get stronger—it has to do with what happened to the place where they were born—but is that all…?

"Lammis, do you…want revenge?"

"Yup. I have to kill the one who attacked our village that day, or I can never forgive myself!"

Hearing a violent word like *kill* come from Lammis's mouth makes my mechanical parts squeak. She was clearly furious when I was kidnapped, but seeing her hate-filled eyes is threatening to break my Heat-Retention feature.

The monsters destroyed their village, as the story goes. Is "the one" she's talking about their boss?

"You mean the guy you said you saw controlling the monsters?"

"That man, he was *smiling* as he controlled them! He was smiling when he killed Ma and Pa, too!"

She pounds the ground with a fist, and it digs into the dirt up to her wrist.

The reason she keeps the ill-fitting hunter occupation has been revealed. I'm sure there are some who would say revenge won't bring back the dead; that it's a fruitless endeavor.

I'm in no position to pretend I know what I'm talking about, and I've never experienced anything like this before. If I'm allowed to give my two cents, however, I'd prefer she strike any bloodthirsty inclinations from her hunter occupation.

But her emotions are something only she understands. I can sympathize, but I can never truly understand, so I want to let her do as she wishes until she's satisfied. And I won't spare an ounce of effort as a vending machine to that end, either.

"Nothing more for me to say, then. We just have to believe the

Menagerie of Fools can handle whatever comes up. Plus, we've got a reliable partner with us now."

A smile appears on Hulemy's lips as she casts a sidelong glance at me. I reply with a confident "Welcome." It's the same volume as her voice, though, so I'm not sure if the feeling got across.

"Thanks for worrying about me, Hulemy. And thank you, too, Boxxo."

Lammis bashfully scratches her head, ashamed of having gotten riled up. As long as I'm on her back, I can protect her with Force Field, but isn't there some other way I can help during battle?

I've absorbed a lot of coins from the thieves' trove, so I have an impressive number of points, but not enough to learn another Blessing. Even if I had the right amount, I'd want to have enough of a safe zone, since there's no telling what could happen. The kidnapping incident taught me that well.

If I want an ability, it'll have to be a single feature. There are several candidates, but they're all really expensive, so I'm hesitant to get any. If I pour tens of thousands of points into a feature that doesn't work the way I thought it would, I'll probably be depressed for a while.

"Let's quit worrying over every little rat in the pack. We still have time before spring anyway. It's late, so let's get some sleep. You've got rubble-clearing work tomorrow morning, don't you?"

"Yup. Okay, let's go to sleep! Oh, Boxxo, you can sleep in our tent tonight."

"You get to sleep with two beautiful women. Best night ever, right?"

She's not wrong, but I don't have a human body. There will be no misunderstandings this night.

I look around the tent again, but the inside is so big that a sizable vending machine being in here doesn't cramp it. A single pillar stands in the circular center, supporting the tent's roof section. It's quite well-made and seems more comfortable to be in than I thought it would be.

Inside the space are two dressers and beds, and a sturdy-looking table with a broad, wooden countertop. Tools and trinkets that look like magic items litter the floor as well. Those have to be Hulemy's.

The room is drab, considering two girls are living in it, but the carnation sitting on the table allows the room to barely pass as effeminate. I'm glad I gave her that gift.

"Oh, and I'm taking good care of the flower you gave me, Boxxo."

"Really? You gave Lammis a present, did you? And it was my birthday three days ago, too. Come to think of it, nobody gave *me* anything."

"Ahh! I'm sorry, I totally forgot. Let's go out to eat and have something delicious tomorrow!"

"Thanks, Lammis. And you, Boxxo—anything for me?"

I'm sure she's half joking, but her smarts are invaluable to me, and I want to rely on her in the future. I actually already know exactly what kinds of things she would like.

The issue is that if I give these things to anyone else, they could be used for evil. I've been waiting for a chance to give them to her without alerting anyone nearby. This situation fits the bill nicely.

"Just kidding. Don't take it so seriously— *Aaahhhh!* What's all this?!"

After transforming into a long and slender body painted in red and white, Hulemy grabs on as though embracing me. Her eyes glitter like a blazing fire, and she begins to breathe violently.

Those eyes are scary! I knew she'd bite, but I didn't think she'd react like this.

"There's all kinds of tools on the other side of the glass. Ah, they're all types I bet Hulemy would like."

Yes. This time, I turned into a vending machine that sells tools. My product lineup consists of safety goggles, masks, convex measuring tape, gloves, an eight-piece screwdriver set, and a hooded nylon jacket, excellent at repelling water.

This vending machine was specifically for hardware stores, so the products are all high quality. Even the gloves have antibacterial deodorizing effects, breathe well, and have nonslip surfaces. Hulemy would probably pay an arm and a leg for something so incredible.

"Hey, how much do they cost?! Lammis, if I don't have enough, lend me some money!"

"Huh? Uh, okay."

The force of Hulemy's bloodshot eyes is overpowering Lammis. I know I could sell these sorts of things to craftsmen, too, but I need to consider the level of technology that's actually safe to introduce here. That's why I only really stock consumable goods.

I trust Hulemy not to use them for anything sinister, so I don't have any qualms about giving them to her.

I know how much money you have on hand, but it's a birthday present this time, so I won't take your money.

I drop a complete set of the items into my compartment, and Hulemy snatches them all up, holds them toward the sky, and squeals in delight. Lammis backs away slowly.

"Boxxo, can I seriously have these for free?!"

"Welcome."

"Thank you so much! I love you!"

Overcome with emotion, Hulemy presses her lips to my glass, then spins around to line up the tools on the table and test them... Wow, that was a surprise. I didn't think she'd actually kiss me. It's tough not having a sense of touch at times like these. N-not that I'm upset or anything.

"Boxxo, you sure seem happy..."

What on earth are you saying, my good Lammis? Why are you glaring at me with those narrowed eyes?

"Hmm..." Her cheeks puff out as she sulks. That's pretty cute, too— Wait, now isn't the time to be content as an observer.

After that, in order to get her out of the bad mood, I give her a bunch of different things I think she'd like as presents, but she continues to pout for the rest of the day.

Vanity, Pride, and Vending Machines, Part 1

"Sir Boxxo, Lady Hulemy, we come bearing a humble request!"

One day, following my usual wave of afternoon customers, I find myself shooting the breeze in front of the Hunters Association building with Hulemy. While she's gushing to me about magic items, we're suddenly surrounded by a group of people in black clothing and sunglasses.

Before we can fully assess the situation, they all bow their heads to us.

Their unique appearances gave them away immediately as Suori's bodyguards, but I wish I knew what sort of "humble request" they were talking about.

"Hey! What's going on here? If you don't explain yourselves properly, you'll just annoy Boxxo."

Yes, that's exactly what I wanted to say. Thanks, Hulemy.

"Please excuse me. In less than an hour from now, we believe the young lady Suori will approach you with a request. We would like you to kindly accept it when she does."

"And what would that request be?"

Rather than provide a straightforward answer to Hulemy's easy question, the bodyguards huddle up in a circle and deliberate their response.

"We request that you keep what you're about to hear a secret. In the very near future, influential merchants will come together for an exhibition where they will show off their personal magic items and respective magic-item engineers."

This situation seems similar to how some nobles have personal artists. So a bunch of rich people are getting together for a show-offy competition with the magic items their engineers made, huh?

"Were the master of the house here, we wouldn't have a problem, but he is currently abroad on business matters and is unable to return for the moment. In a stroke of bad luck, his personal engineer is with him as well, so we have no engineers to participate with."

"And you thought Boxxo and I would fit the bill?"

Hulemy's remark seems to be right on the money, and the whole crowd bows to us at once.

But if that "master of the house" or whatever isn't around, can't they just not attend?

"If the higher-ups aren't here, why don't you just sit this one out?"

Hulemy's thoughts are so in line with mine that it's scary. I think it's a coincidence, but… She didn't actually complete that mind-reading magic item from a while back, did she?

"Unfortunately, this event was planned by the daughter of a merchant who seems to have some sort of quarrel with the young lady… She will be attending in place of her parents as well, which means the young lady must attend…"

"A competition of vanity. Rich people really have it rough, huh?"

The black-clad bodyguards fidget remorsefully at Hulemy's sarcasm.

I've got a better grasp the situation now, but what should we do? Suori is one of my loyal customers, so I wouldn't mind participating, but I don't think Hulemy has ever even met her.

"The young lady Suori has a somewhat…a bit of a…a rather *intractable* personality, so we believe her interactions with you may become overbearing before long."

Yep, I agree with you there. I can easily imagine that. Was that why they got in touch with me in advance?

"Therefore, we ask you to please— What? The young lady is close?! This is far sooner than we expected. Please, keep our meeting a secret!"

No sooner had a woman in black whispered something into the

man's ear than did they scatter like spiderlings and vanish; not unlike ninjas.

"Um, well... Those guys sure have it rough, huh?"

"Welcome."

"The young lady Suori. I've seen her buying things from you a few times. She's the real tiny one, right?"

"Welcome." Yes, yes. It's the strong-willed girl with the twin-tails.

For a while after our reunion, she had a bad attitude. She would constantly try to pull pranks on me—though they all ended in failure.

She's not actually that bad of a kid, and it seemed like she was going through some personal drama at the time, so that probably influenced her behavior even further.

Speak of the devil, here she comes.

As always, her gait is proud and bold, but her usually firm glare is darting all over the place. She seems nervous.

Spotting Hulemy drinking a milk tea next to me, Suori's eyes widen for just a moment.

After walking up to me, she looks between Hulemy and me.

I know it's hard for her to find the words right now, but instead of words, a silent pressure flows from within her, a force of will you'd expect from someone much older.

"E-excuse me... Would you happen to be the famous magic-item engineer, Hulemy?"

When she talks like this, she looks like your standard, proper young lady. It feels weird to me, though, considering her usual cheeky attitude.

"Yep, that's me. And who might you be, miss?"

"Please excuse my rudeness. I'm— My name is Suori. I understand this may be ill-mannered of me, but I have something I'd like to request from you, Lady Hulemy, and you, Sir Boxxo."

It looks like she's prepared herself. Her serious gaze pierces Hulemy and me.

"I do not mind if it is only temporary, but would you please help me and play the role as my personal magic-item engineer and her invention?!"

The little ball of pride and conceit is now bowing deeply to us. That must be how important this is to her.

The black-clad bodyguards, watching us from behind buildings, put hands to their mouths, clearly unsettled.

"Oh, quit it. Kids aren't supposed to do that. Lift your head back up."

"Th-then may I take this to mean that you accept?"

"Well, if you have a good reason, I'll think about it. But only if you stop with that hoity-toity way of speaking and talk naturally. Right, Boxxo?" Hulemy says with a wink.

Suori fixes her stare upon Hulemy as if she's a rare animal. This must be her first time interacting with someone like her.

"U-um, do you promise you won't get mad if my tone is slightly rougher?"

"Kids are supposed to be a little cheeky."

"Well, then. Hulemy, Boxxo, could you please help me?"

Yep, there's the tone I'm so familiar with. Time to hear her real thoughts on the matter.

"There's a rival shop our business has been in competition with for some time. The heiress is this bratty girl who has a bad personality, looks at you funny, and talks weird. And she's ugly! She shamelessly decided to have an exhibition right when she knew my father wasn't here. Just thinking about that detestable face of hers makes me want to... Grrrr!"

Now she's stomping on the ground. Could it possibly involve some past event that makes her blood seethe just by remembering it?

Hulemy's face is drawn back from Suori's sudden change in attitude.

"Oh my, I do apologize. This exhibition involves bringing one's personal magic-item engineer as well as their creations, and...bragging about them, if we're being honest. It's a rubbish gathering, really."

Wait, Suori doesn't think highly of the gathering? That's a surprise.

"Nevertheless, should I refuse, my father's prestige will hit rock bottom. As his daughter, I must rub that egotistical brat's face into the mud, or I won't be satisfied."

They must really not like each other. The sinister grin on Suori's face is something I've never seen on a little kid before. Rather than save face as a merchant, it seems like she really just doesn't want to lose.

"What do you say? I can make it worth your while. Will you help me?"

I don't have a problem with helping—in fact, now I'm interested, so I was already going to accept. But what about Hulemy?

I shift my gaze to her to see a smirk on the edges of her lips... Oh, this should be fun. She's thinking the same thing as I am, isn't she?

"Sure, sounds good. This oughtta be fun. I accept."

Now that she's cheerfully consented, my own answer is easy. "Welcome."

"Thank you very much!"

Suori's smile is like a blooming flower, revealing a cuteness appropriate for her age, making me feel happy just looking at it.

I don't know what lies in store for us, but to be honest, I'm sort of looking forward to it.

Several days passed after that, and I was eventually brought to a specially installed tent.

I'd been excited, thinking we might be going outside the dungeon, but Suori wouldn't be leaving this stratum on her own, either, so the exhibition took place inside a temporary tent hastily assembled for the occasion.

I call it a tent, but it's fashioned from an elaborately designed fabric, and to be blunt, it really stands out against the rest of the Clearflow Lake stratum that's currently being rebuilt.

The interior design is simple, but a skillfully made carpet covers the ground, no doubt a show of how rich they are.

Currently, I'm snuggled up in a big tarp, with only a small hole out of which I can secure a field of vision. My range of sight is not good by any stretch of the imagination.

"Boxxo, can you see?"

"Welcome."

That must be Hulemy next to me, whispering out of consideration.

The story today is that I'm a brand-new magic item created by the magic-item engineer, Hulemy.

She has plenty to be proud of already with her sheer fame and skill as an engineer, but she must really want to give this young lady a thrashing. I'm not trying to brag, either, but I don't think any normal magic items will be a match for me and my vending machine capabilities. I start to feel sorry for Suori's adversary.

Right now, we're waiting in a corner of the tent for this so-called exhibition to start. People who look like magic-item engineers shuffle in one after another, objects covered in cloth carried in right behind them.

It looks like there are a total of five magic items, if the cloths are any indication. Next to us are a man and woman in white scientist-type clothing. They must be magic-item engineers.

The cloth-covered objects come in many sizes, some not half my height, one twice as big as I am.

I've seen a tent like this, specially installed at a venue, once before as a child—and I understand now why they needed something as large as a circus tent.

We're in one of its corners, but in the middle section is a cluster of people, old and young, male and female, wearing the kind of rich-person clothes you'd see in paintings and having pleasant chats with one another.

Suori is in there, too. Now, I wonder where this "detestable" young lady is. If she's close in age, I should be able to spot her right—there she is.

Her height is about the same, too, and her clothing is of similar design. Suori's outfit is mainly red, but hers uses blues. Her hair is silver and straight, reaching down to her ankles, while her skin is fair like high-quality Japanese paper. Her eyes are narrow, with the corners angled slightly down, making her appear docile. Even when she laughs, she puts a hand to her mouth with a refined gesture, radiating a prettiness that is exactly the opposite of the energetic Suori.

At a glance, it looks like Suori has lost the "young lady" competition, but I won't say that.

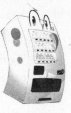

The idle talk among rich folks is livening up. Can we please just start the exhibition already?

Next to me, Hulemy, seeming equally bored, opens her mouth wide and yawns. Suori seems used to this, as she wonderfully feigns friendliness, pretending to be a well-bred young lady.

She's even exchanging pleasantries with the girl in the blue dress. If they're trying to maintain appearances, they're both doing an excellent job of hiding what they really think.

Oh, and as I think that, Suori and her rival bow gracefully to the adults and head this way.

As they get closer, I'm able to make out their faces more clearly, and...yeah, they're definitely not friends.

They may look like they're smiling at each other, but both their cheeks are twitching. I can also hear them now.

"Mistress Suori, you needn't have pushed yourself. You could have just twiddled your thumbs and watched in envy this time around."

"Oh-ho-ho-ho. I could never do something like that. Mistress Kanashi, you, on the other hand, have such a frail constitution, so please, don't force yourself. It would pain my conscience deeply if you had a heart attack out of shock."

"Oh my, but how could it pain your conscience if you don't have one?"

"Ufu-fu-fu. I knew about your stature and personality, but are your ears poor as well? How troublesome."

Their conversation is riddled with so many thorns, I can scarcely believe I'm listening to children.

Their shoulders and foreheads jab into each other as they arrive in front of me. Unfortunately, I can't see Hulemy's expression, but I'm sure she's grimacing.

"Come to think of it, Mistress Suori, is this the magic-item engineer you so hastily dug up?"

"Yes, that's right. She's incredibly talented, and her magic item is stunningly high quality. It doesn't even compare to yours—no, even to compare it would be a pity."

Wow, she's brimming with confidence. She seems to really trust Hulemy and me.

The other young lady—the one called Kanashi—appears calm, but the eyes looking out from her thinly opened lids are anything but amicable.

"H-hmm. A female magic-item engineer? She does look intelligent, but... Well, no matter. Please, boast all you like while you still have the chance. I will look forward to your hopelessly frustrated face anon."

If she had given a high-pitched laugh and walked away, it would have been perfect, but she seems to be holding back since others are watching.

"Ahhh, she makes me so mad! I'm terribly sorry to make you two uncomfortable."

"Well, actually, your conversation was interesting."

"Welcome."

If it had been two adult women saying those things to each other, I might have felt fear. But the two of them being adorable girls makes me want to cheer them on, like I'm watching them attempt a performance beyond their abilities.

"I'm sorry for showing you something so distasteful. It looks like the time is near. Please wait here until it's our turn."

We don't have anything to do while we wait, so I turn my ear to Hulemy's talk of magic items until a man in tuxedo-like clothing exits through the back of the tent. He spreads his arms wide.

"Ladies and gentlemen, welcome, and thank you for coming. By your leave, I shall omit any needless preface. We will now begin the exhibition."

He must be the moderator. Now I can relax and watch until it's our turn.

They apparently decided on an order beforehand; a person in black comes up to us and whispers that we'll be last in line.

The first to display is a plump man with the archetypal rich-person assortment of accessories, notably the rings on every finger. Next to him is a man in white clothing who looks high-strung, slender, and lanky compared with his companion. He must be their magic-item engineer.

They remove the cloth covering the magic item to reveal a... What is that? A circular pillar that only reaches up to a person's waist, and its diameter is about the size of your palm. At a glance, it looks like a club that would be hard to use. A finicky weapon—it's too short, and it's fat besides. What kind of magic item is it?

"What sort of magic item is this?"

"This? This is a magic item that can transform into a variety of weapons."

Oh! A magic item to tickle my boyish fancies.

"Really, now?" says Hulemy, her voice animated. Anything magic item–related seems to get her going. "I thought of something like that once, too. This should be good."

The lanky magic-item engineer places it on a pedestal and does something with it. A split appears in the pillar, and it begins to transform. He inserts a hilt-like object into the side, and the pillar section splits apart and reforms, changing into an ax.

Next, the ax becomes a great sword, and then a spear. Its edge is sharp as any blade, equal to general weapons.

However, the crowd's reaction is weak. Hulemy, too, just heaves a sigh. She doesn't say a word. She must think it absurd.

And with good reason. This magic item could sell well as a multipurpose weapon, if it could split apart and reform automatically. But everything is done by hand... You have to disassemble it yourself, then reassemble it like a puzzle.

I feel waves of sorrow coming off the magic-item engineer as he desperately builds it.

The second, third, and fourth people up didn't have anything too unusual—they were all better versions of things sold in stores. According to Hulemy's interpretations anyway.

"Oh, right. That young lady's magic item was up second to last, right? She seemed pretty confident. Let's go have a look."

The magic items thus far have been pretty lame. Is it okay to get my hopes up, just a little?

"Would you mind if I came to see as well?" asks Suori. "I'd like your instruction, Miss Hulemy."

"Sure thing. It's more fun to see stuff like this together."

Whatever she may say, Suori seems interested too as she stares at Kanashi.

Her magic-item engineer is both tall and muscular; his white robe looks like it's about to burst at the seams. With a constitution like that, he'd probably be more suited to hunting than engineering pursuits.

Their magic item is relatively big, about the same size as the well-built engineer. Now I'm really getting my hopes up. What could be under that cloth?

"Well then, allow me to explain. First, have a look."

He takes the cloth off to reveal a golden doll. It looks like two red jewels are fitted into its head as eyes. Aside from that, it doesn't look like any more than a female mannequin painted gold.

To be quite honest, it shows a complete lack of any design sensibilities.

"As I'm sure you are all aware, there exist several fiends that resemble the human form, such as wood fiends, crag fiends, and earth fiends. This magic item was born from that idea—a work of art that will obey a person's orders."

In other words, a golem, as they come up in fantasy. They're famous for being magical creatures created by humans. I thought there would already be something like that in this world, but I guess there isn't.

Come to think of it, when I first met Hulemy, she mentioned the impossibility of granting intelligence to a magic item. Remembering that, I look over to her and see her casting a dangerously sharp glare at the golden mannequin.

"Could that guy have...?" she mutters lowly.

I've got a bad feeling about this, but I have no way to ask, so I just need to be cautious of the mannequin.

"An intelligent magic item has long been the dream of magic-item engineers. And I have realized this dream! But they say actions speak louder than words. I will turn it on now, so please see it with your own eyes."

He goes behind the vulgar gold mannequin, fiddles with something on its back, and its red eyes light up.

The mannequin, before standing completely still, slowly lifts one arm up, places it at its chest, and bows, earning an immediate murmur of admiration from the crowd.

"Suori, if something happens, stay with Boxxo. And call your friend over here, too."

"Wh-why should I have to call Kanashi—?"

"If you don't want her to die, get her over here. Boxxo, protect them if you need to."

Suori tried to object, but upon realizing the danger after seeing Hulemy's face, she swallowed it back down.

"If my fears are unfounded, everything will be fine. But if they're right...things could get bad."

"I...I understand. I don't know what's going on, but allowing her to be hurt would harm my dignity as her superior. I'll be right back."

"Quickly, if you can."

Suori slowly nods before running over to Kanashi, who has been sending the occasional pride-filled glance our way.

"Boxxo, you remember when I told you it's impossible to plant intelligence in a magic item?"

"Welcome."

"Technology like that is still undiscovered. If you implant one with a human soul, it's in the realm of possibility. But it's so dangerous that the Magic-Item Engineering Society forbade it. There was a fool of a magic-item engineer before who implanted a giant rock puppet with a human soul, thinking it would be a powerful soldier if they could control it at will. Long story short, they couldn't, and it destroyed a town."

In other words, there's a high chance this engineer violated taboo. Which is why Hulemy's on her guard. We have to consider the worst case, that it goes out of control.

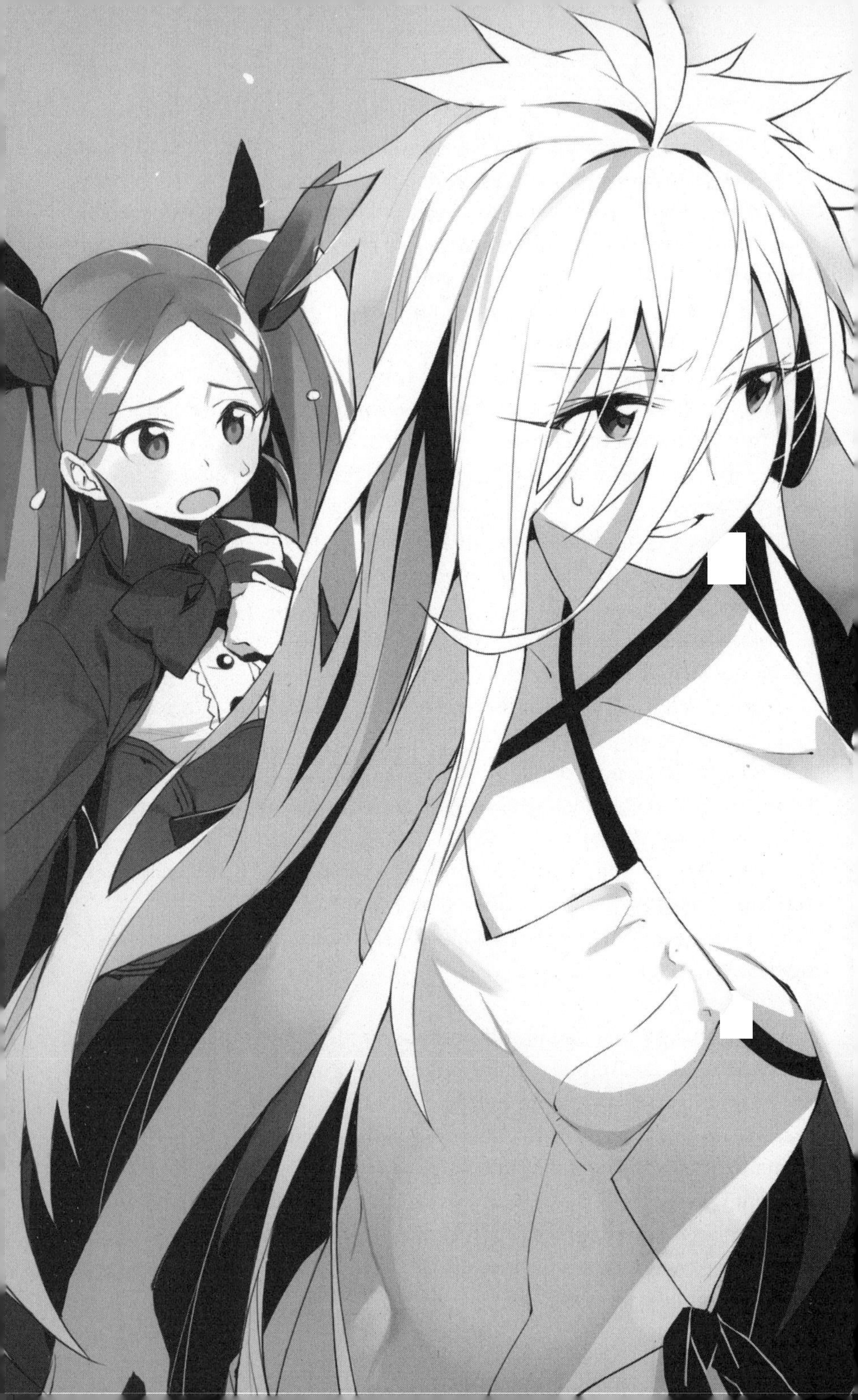

"Of course, if he's more talented than I am, we won't have a problem."

A better engineer than Hulemy? I know she's capable, but I still don't have a handle on her level relative to others in this world. I've never had anyone to compare her to.

Wait, I have to pay attention. Observing the mannequin's movements is more important than idle speculation.

At the man's instructions, the mannequin walks, jumps, carries, and performs basic martial arts movements. To my amateur's eyes, the movements seem smooth, like this engineer has done it well.

"What do you think of this wonderful magic item, everyone? It will obediently carry out your orders with excellence, never turning on you."

He's gloating. He spreads his arms wide, speaking fervently.

"Mistress Suori, what do you think of the magic item we produced? A moving magical doll that understands human words!"

It looks like she managed to get Kanashi over here. Suori ignores her stream of boasts, somehow holding herself back from arguing.

She seems to find Kanashi annoying, but she is worried about her. She's got a bad mouth, but she's a nice kid at heart. She's pretty similar to Hulemy, actually.

Words of praise fly from the spectators as the mannequin obediently kneels next to the delighted engineer, awaiting its next orders.

It would be great if nothing else happened.

"IL... KI...LL..."

Wait, whose voice was that?

"Oh, he explained previously that it wasn't able to speak," says Kanashi. "He must have been keeping it secret. What a nice surprise that is!"

"It's not nice at all," says Hulemy. "Dammit, I was right. Both of you, stay right there. Don't move."

"All right," says Suori.

"What? Huh? What's going on?" says Kanashi, the conversation proceeding without her understanding the situation.

The air around Hulemy is tense. Her worst-case prediction must have come true.

"KIL...L...SOMEO...NE... KI...LL..."

"Wh-what's wrong?" stammers the engineer. "I didn't give it the powers of speech. What is going on? I...I have to stop it!"

The engineer goes around behind the golden mannequin and fiddles with something. As he does, the mannequin's head spins around and looks at him.

"N-nooo! I pressed the emergency shutdown button! Why won't you stop?!"

"ARE YOU…THE ONE…WHO AWOKE ME FROM MY SLUMBER?!"

A cry of despair from the mannequin fills the entire tent.

The large magic-item engineer is backing off, seeming dumbfounded, but the mannequin edges toward him, one arm hanging in front of it.

"You idiot!" shouts Hulemy. "Did you seal a human soul inside a puppet by force?! Hey, you, in the black clothes—go hold that thing down! I'll handle the rest somehow!"

The black-clad bodyguards are flabbergasted, but they immediately remember their duty. They all jump on the mannequin at once, quickly binding its arms and legs, pinning it to the ground.

They are bodyguards, after all. They seem accustomed to this.

Hulemy places a hand on a round gem on the berserk mannequin's back, then exhales. "Preventing a soul's escape with a magic circle, and even using a brainwashing spell… You piece of shit. You're a defiler of the dead!"

Hulemy, enraged, glares at the magic-item engineer. His face grows pale.

"It must have been so hard…," she continues to the mannequin. "Sorry for waking you up. None of this is your fault. This time, you can rest in peace."

As she whispers gently, her fingers trace something atop the gem. A moment later, the berserk mannequin's head stops, and the red lights in its eyes go out.

"We can rest easy now. I undid the restraints and released the soul. It won't ever move again."

"N-no! I spent so many years on this research and finally came up with this technique! You couldn't possibly undo it after a cursory glance!"

The magic-item engineer, unable to accept the facts, drops to his knees and sprays spittle everywhere as he cries out.

"Ha. Big talk for someone who used such a crude method. In the hands of Hulemy, it's weaker than a baby frog fiend."

That's an extreme analogy, but I recall it being an expression in this world. Frog-fiend children are similar to tadpoles, with no combat power, weak enough that even children could stomp them out.

"H-Hulemy?! Mayhem's Prodigy Hulemy?!"

"Don't call me that."

All the magic-item engineers in attendance seem shocked at the man's outburst. She must be pretty famous in the industry.

"Hulemy? You mean the problem child who caused several explosions and small fires in her time at the School of Magic-Item Engineering? Though her grades were apparently excellent."

"The rumors say she once made a sleeping drug that was so strong, it knocked out everyone at the school."

"I heard she developed a chemical to purify water, and when she poured it into a dirty lake, it not only purified it, but evaporated all the water!"

Hulemy can hear the engineers talking, and she steadily grows redder and redder.

Would you knock it off already? Please, stop exposing the shame of her younger years!

In the end, the mannequin was broken to pieces, and the engineer responsible was escorted out by the guards.

The famous Hulemy—for better or worse—has a crowd of admirers around her now. Looking at her embarrassed-yet-happy expression makes me feel like that alone makes the commotion worth it.

There's something to be said for Suori, too, as others lavish her with praise for the personal magic-item engineer she employed. With a huge grin on her face, she speaks to Kanashi, who bites a handkerchief in frustration.

The commotion was annoying, but they've accepted Hulemy, and Suori seems satisfied, so I think we can deem our mission a success.

The only unresolved matter is—well, the cloth is still covering me. Do I not get a chance to show off? Hey, did you all forget about something?

Canned Oden

Winters in the Clearflow Lake stratum are fairly severe, and while not as bad as regions of heavy snowfall in Japan, there is still a constant two-inch layer of snow on the ground. If more snow fell, the tents would be in danger of collapsing, so they almost never get more than a couple feet of accumulation… Hopefully anyway.

The monsters on this stratum burrow deep underground to hibernate during the winter, making hunting and material collecting difficult. The gatekeeper Karios, eating a can of oden, explains that the modus operandi is to cloister in the settlement.

This year, however, the reconstruction efforts mean the settlement has no want for work. Even the hunters who usually move to a different stratum once winter comes are staying here. I remember the young merchant happily telling me, with a milk tea in one hand, that it's a good time to turn a profit.

I've fallen into a pattern of stocking only drinks until the eateries close up shop for the day, then bringing out foods to join them after. I understand the outside air is very cold, but since I don't have any temperature-sensing features, it doesn't bother me at all.

Oh, but maybe I *should* add one that can measure the temperature. More advanced vending machines, so called next-generation ones, can gauge the temperature and even display recommended items.

As for points... That's not too much. Maybe I should choose it.

"Phew, it's cold out. Time for some soup and a hot meal."

Few are curious enough to buy my products after night has set and the frigid winds are blustering. Considering the familiar voice, this is doubtlessly Karios, a gatekeeper.

"Gorth, what are you getting today?"

"Sweet tea."

"That's all you ever get."

"And cooked food on a skewer is all you ever get."

Karios and Gorth must be on gate duty today. It's pretty commendable that they work so hard, even in cold weather. After they buy their warmed items, they like to put them in their inside pockets for a while for warmth, so I set them to be a little hotter than normal.

"Piping hot, as always. Thanks, Boxxo."

"My thanks."

"Thank you," I reply. They've seemed to realize I'm adjusting the heat in consideration of them, so they always thank me.

These two might be the ones I've talked to the most after coming to this settlement, except for Lammis. Well, it's more like Karios rattles on and on, leaving Gorth and me to follow along idly.

They arch their backs, and with their thick coat collars up, they disappear into the dark. When I see them like that, it makes me want to set up closer to the gate, but Lammis refuses to be any farther from me, so I seldom move away from my normal spot with the girls' tent in view.

After seeing the two regulars off, something red slides into the corner of my vision.

Here we go again.

It's a woman wearing a dress as red as blood. Not a short-sleeved dress, mind you, but a long one with baggy sleeves. She's probably bundled up underneath that. The scarf around her neck is scarlet as well, with her shoes and gloves equally crimson in color. I can't get a good view of her face, though. Her long black hair reaches down to her waist, and her bangs hang down to the tip of her nose. Her mouth is the only thing I can see, her lips dyed rouge.

The woman stands idly, an eerie drop of red against the midnight darkness. Normally, one might understandably cry out and run away, but I can't move, nor do any of my features let me scream.

More importantly, I've gotten used to her.

She shows up pretty frequently—and always at night.

A nighttime regular is unusual by itself, and her clothes only add to it. I'd remember her even if I didn't want to.

I feel it's dangerous for a woman to walk around alone at night, but if you asked me if anyone had the courage to speak up to her, I don't know if I could answer.

As always, after buying a can of oden, she slips back into the darkness.

I've already reincarnated as a vending machine. It wouldn't be strange for ghosts to exist. Still, she has a physical form—she's actually alive. And the moment she picks up the can of oden, a smile tugs at her lips. Maybe she's crazy for the stuff.

My customers are my customers, no matter what kind of people they are. And she makes it a little less lonely for me when I'm out here all by my mechanized self.

Still, it really seems like it'll be cold today.

"Phew. Why do we have to be on duty on such a miserably cold night?"

"Give it a rest."

The shaven Karios and the crew-cut Gorth are on the lookout again tonight, it seems. They're particularly skilled among the rest of the settlement's guards, so they're frequently assigned to night shifts, when terrible monsters have a higher chance of appearing.

"It's so cold. Should've put on another scarf."

"Your taste in color is awful as always."

"Ha! Shows what you know. Red's my lucky color. Had a trusted conjurer tell me once."

I'm honestly not sure about a red scarf on a rugged guy, but everyone has their own likes and dislikes. What's most important is that a person wears what they like.

"Speaking of red, you hear those rumors?"

"Yeah, the one about the scarlet ghost lady? I hear people have been spotting her late at night recently. We'll have to get rid of her if she's a harmful ghost, though."

Ghosts are objects of fear in this world, too—but can you hunt them? I should have expected as much from an alternate world. I don't see a hint of fear in either of these two.

The rumored ghost must be that woman. I thought she was a ghost the first time, too, so I can understand why gossip about her is making the rounds.

The pair of guards buy their usual cans of oden and milk tea, then head swiftly toward the gate. A moment before they go out of sight, the usual woman in red comes into view.

This may be late in coming, but I've noticed a pattern to when she shows up. She always comes here right after those two guards appear. Then, clutching a can of oden, she disappears in the direction of the gate, as though following them.

Even I have enough information to realize what's going on. The woman in red clothes has a thing for Karios. She buys oden, his favorite product, and puts together red outfits, a color he said he liked.

She comes off as a bit of a stalker, which is scary, but if she's watching him from afar, there shouldn't be a problem...I think.

As I observe her closely, a gust of cold wind blows through, whipping her bangs up. One look at the face underneath and I gasp.

Clear eyes and a perfect nose. Her lips are painted red in an unembellished yet very charming expression—so charming I accidentally record it on my vending machine surveillance camera.

"Sir Karios..."

I hear her voice for the first time, seemingly fragile and nearly carried away on the night breeze, but I can sense the passion in her words.

I don't believe Karios has a lover or a wife. If she really made an advance on him, I think he'd fall for her, but she doesn't appear to have the courage. Besides, it depends on his own tastes, so I suppose all I can do is watch over them warmly.

Clutching her can of oden in her hands, she again heads off in the direction of the gate, as though wandering after Karios.

* * *

"Right, we're off duty today! What should I do?"

Karios raises his voice, giddy enough to break into a skip as he appears in front of me. This is the first time I've seen him in normal clothing, and they're, well, normal. Save for the red scarf anyway, which sticks out like a sore thumb, reminding me of the first of those old *kamen*-whatevers.

"Why not buy some equipment at that furniture shop?"

Gorth seems to be on his way to his post, so he's in his usual attire. He buys a milk tea.

"Oh, y-you're right. If you say so. To the furniture shop!"

Hmm? He's starting to fidget for some reason. He stares at himself in my glass, checking to see if his clothes are wrinkled.

Gorth, watching him, smirks and says, "Heh."

"A-all right, maybe I'll get a souvenir for... Oh!"

"O-oh, hello, Karios."

Karios sees a woman passing through by chance and his back immediately straightens up. The woman, too, stiffens, holding bags in both arms.

"Wh-what a coincidence. I was just about to head to the furniture store."

"I—I see. I was just heading back there myself. Oh, that's quite the beautiful red scarf you have."

"I see. I actually quite like red."

Karios's polite tone feels completely wrong. Despite the cold weather, sweat begins to form on his brow and temples. He seems pretty nervous.

The woman's eyes are wandering as well, making her seem rather suspicious. Wait, could these two be tog— Oh, her face... I know that face. She's holding her bangs out of her face with an Alice band, so I can see it clearly. It's that woman in the red clothes. I compared it with the image on my surveillance camera, and there's no doubt.

Wait, is this an honest-to-goodness case of mutual interest? I want to wish them well, but at the same time, it makes me a little mad for some reason.

"Karios, if you're going to the furniture shop, why not offer to carry her things?"

Oh, good one, Gorth.

"Y-yeah. If it pleases you, I'll carry your things."

"Th-thank you very much."

He takes her bags, and the two walk away side by side. As he watches their backs, Gorth heaves a sigh. "Good grief. They should just start dating already."

"Welcome." I think so, too. I make my agreement known.

Late that night, as the usual pair leaves me, the blur of red—the furniture shop lady—appears. As always, she clutches her can of oden, gazing after Karios.

"Sir Karios, how can I make my feelings known to you?"

The definition of a maiden in love.

According to Gorth, Karios rescued her just as a belligerent hunter was dragging her into the dark in the settlement not too long ago.

She started talking to him after that, and before he knew it, Karios had seriously fallen for her. Despite his hearty nature, he was apparently slow to mature when it came to women, and couldn't get himself to take the first step, a behavior that had persisted to this day.

Hmm. A chance? The best option is for the man to take the lead, but with such a stern appearance and his nerves around women, he won't be able to talk about much.

But if there was a reason for the woman to make the approach...

Hmm, yeah, that might work.

She sighs. "Once again, I've dressed myself in your favorite red today, and yet I can do naught but watch as you leave... Oh?"

I ignore her soliloquy and change my body's shape—to a vending machine I once saw selling vegetables at an eatery.

"Are these vegetables?"

As she looks at me, confused, I open up my glass-paned, locker-like lid to reveal several daikon radishes.

"I, huh? Can I take these?"

"Welcome."

After watching her nervously take the daikon radish, I change into my egg-vending mode. I provide her with a pack of eggs in the same way.

Then I drop a *chikuwa* fish cake into my compartment. Not that it matters at the moment, but the myriad of products available from vending machines amazes me. I spotted this one in a certain parking lot.

Finally, I return to my normal vending machine mode, then stock my shelves with a certain item I'm very fond of, despite it making me look crazy. Plastic bottles full of fish broth.

I discovered this vending machine in Osaka, and the pricier items in it were flying fish–based broth, known as *ago-dashi*. An entire fish goes into each bottle of it.

"U-um, well, what would you have me do with all this?"

For the finisher, I drop a can of oden into my compartment. When she sees it, her eyes open wide in surprise at me. She must have realized.

"You want me to make a stew out of these ingredients, don't you?"

"Welcome."

"Th-thank you very much! I'll use this to make him notice me!"

Understanding everything, she thanks me several times, then runs off in the opposite direction from the gate. As I watch her single-minded zeal, I hope things go well, but the thought of spring coming for Karios irritates me a little. I suppose I can't help it.

"Gorth, Boxxo, love is great! Every day shines like the sun! Oh, right, get this—yesterday, she made me a home-cooked meal again, and it was amazing!"

A few days after the woman invited Karios to eat her homemade oden, the distance between them suddenly closed and they started going out. Ever since then, Gorth and I have had to sit through his amorous boasting.

Gorth looks at him with cold eyes and an incredibly disdainful expression, but Karios is blissfully unaware. I have to give him credit—every time I see him, he's able to go on and on about his lady friend without getting bored. It's not just a little annoying—it's extremely aggravating.

I'm starting to regret bringing them together a little.

"Yeah, it was great. Oh, looks like the watch shifts change soon. I'll have the same thing as always. It's not as good as her cooking, but it's good in its own way!"

Gleeful, Karios buys a can of oden like always and goes to pick it up.

"*Heeyah!* It's cold! Wh-what's this? Boxxo, it's not warm!"

Pfft. Enjoy your chilled oden.

Spring Comes

"Karios, your collar is crooked."

"O-oh. Thanks. I think I'll be back late tonight. Don't cry because you're lonely."

"I won't. I'll make your favorite stew with plenty of eggs and wait for you. Please make doubly sure you're not injured."

"It hurts me so much to leave you that it feels like my body is being torn to shreds... But I have a job to do. I'm sorry."

"No, I don't want to part with you, either. But it would pain me if I got in the way of your work. I will fight back the tears, and..."

Could you two *please* give it a rest already?! Day in, day out, the two of you flirt in front of a vending machine like the love-drunk couple that you are.

Look! Even Gorth is face-palming. He's clearly exhausted. They're on duty together a lot, so he must have to hear these stories day in and day out. I pity him.

"Munami, the weather is fine today again. The sunlight has been warming up recently—it's the perfect weather to go for a walk."

"You're right. Will your store be okay without you today?"

The other annoying crew is here. It's the young merchant and the self-titled poster girl of the inn, Munami. They haven't started going out yet, but Munami seems to be talking to him as a friend rather than as a customer, so they're on much better terms than they were before.

And for some reason, every last one of them starts having a conversation in front of me. Sigh. Just when I felt the temperature rising and spring coming on, a bunch of people at the height of their own springs are gathering.

But there's no time to idly bask in the seasons changing, because soon the hunters will start going back to work. That includes Lammis and also reminds me of my promise to the Menagerie of Fools to participate in their expedition...

"Boxxo, how are you doing?"

"Heh, looks like you're selling well as always. It's nice and warm out today, so I'll take a cold fizzling drink."

Speak of the devil, or what have you. Lammis and Hulemy are here.

The couples seem to have left at some point. I'm happy they're friendly, but I really wish they'd do their thing somewhere else. I don't have a physical body, so matters of love have nothing to do with me.

But it's not like I'm j-jealous or anything. Next time I see them, I'll even give them warmed carbonated drinks to celebrate.

"Boxxo, we're set to leave tomorrow," says Lammis. "Are you still okay with this?"

"Welcome." I've known about it for a long time in advance. I don't have a reason to refuse at this point.

I'm racked with worry, but I do hope that she gets stronger. The two of us are like two halves of a whole. All we can do is make up for what the other lacks.

Well, I'm talking pretty big, but I'm the one who lacks a whole lot more in comparison to her. I don't have arms or legs, after all. She's always the one helping me.

"Oh, right, it was tomorrow, wasn't it? That whole thing about you going with the Menagerie of Fools on a job?"

"That's right, Hulemy. I think they said we're going to, um, scope out the crocodile fiends."

"The crocodile fiends—one of the Three Factions dwelling in the Clearflow Lake stratum..."

Like Hulemy says, the monsters dwelling in this stratum can be broadly categorized into three groups. The frog people—or frog fiends. The double serpents, one of which attacked the settlement. And the bipedal lizardmen—no, crocodile people, the crocodile fiends.

The stratum seems to be home to frogs, snakes, and crocodiles. After the frogs and snakes showed up, I remembered an old children's game and assumed the third would be slugs, but it turned out to be crocodiles.

When you think about it, this is a marshy region, so maybe slugs would be out of place.

"We're investigating if the crocodile fiends' numbers have grown now that we beat the frog fiends and the double serpent. Putting them down is secondary—he said we were going to see how much of a threat they might be."

Two of the three major threats have taken serious damage, so if we investigate the crocodiles' habitat and they've gotten too populous, they plan to put together a hunting team.

Strata have their own ecosystems, and it's normal that something odd will happen if you blindly ruin it. The tragedy three years ago was apparently due to the monster factions' equilibrium getting messed up.

"It's true—you'll have to investigate while you have the chance, or it could spell trouble later. We're talking about a king frog fiend and a giant double serpent appearing. Something strange might be happening in this stratum… Lammis, if things get bad, get out of there."

"Yup. If it gets dangerous, I'll take Boxxo and run away. Right?"

"Welcome." I'll remember to be on my guard all throughout the expedition so I can use my Force Field at any time.

Normally, one would need all sorts of preparations, but I don't have anything to do, really. About all I can do is stock some new products and set myself up to provide items depending on the situation. Oh, I should give the stores some ingredients before going.

Also, I'll have to sell my drinks cheap at Munami's temporary inn. I'll be away from the settlement for a while, so if I can provide my regulars with enough to tide them over, I'll be all set.

The entire settlement seems to know we're going on this expedition with the Menagerie of Fools, so people continued to come to me until late at night to stock up.

*   *   *

The next morning, Lammis and Hulemy eat their breakfast next to me.

Lammis has on leather armor and sturdy-looking boots for the expedition, but several small bags also hang from her waist. She also has the wooden rack for carrying me.

I'm here for her food, so that isn't a problem, and I can light up as well. It seems like my Heat-Retention feature works on anyone nearby, so I can dampen both the cold and the warm for her while she sleeps. And if it comes to it, I can just give her a bath towel.

Which means I guess she doesn't need to bring much. She'll be lugging me along too, after all, so she can't exactly bring anything large. The Menagerie of Fools will apparently be providing the bare minimum in terms of items, so I suppose I don't need to worry about much.

"Yo, Lammis, Boxxo. You guys all ready?"

Following that greeting appears Captain Kerioyl, the shady-looking man with some newly acquired length to his stubble, his trademark ten-gallon hat sitting askew on his head. Next to him is the blue-haired vice captain, Filmina, as well.

"Good morning, everyone. If there are no issues, the buar cart is waiting at the gate."

"We're all ready. Boxxo, let's go. Hup, ho!"

She hoists me onto her back as easily as ever, then follows behind the captain and the vice captain. We've been inside the settlement all winter, so it'll be nice to go outside. Lately, I've been feeling less like I'm in an alternate world and more like a set for a fantasy movie.

Few people arm themselves in the winter; most wear plain clothing, which sometimes causes me to forget that I'm in a fantasy world. Of course, Director Bear and others with animal features appeared every once in a while, bringing me back to reality.

In this world, the animal people aren't the fantastical sort—humans with cat ears and tails and such—but actual animals. The frog people are the same. It seems that, in general, it's like they took animals and rearranged their skeletons to be more human-esque.

"Living confined inside the walls starts to make you stir-crazy, doesn't it? You have to go outside and get a breath of fresh air every once in a while, or you'll start to rot."

"Welcome," I reply, only now noticing that Hulemy is walking alongside us. Is she coming to see us off?

"That over there is the Menagerie's buar cart," says Filmina, pointing to a single giant buar with a cart behind it. It's stopped a little farther out than the gate. Karios and Gorth are nearby, having a chat with hunters who seem to be members of the Menagerie.

"Oh, Lammis, Boxxo. Be careful out there, okay? Ah, wait a minute. I want to stock up on a few things."

"I'll buy some things, too."

I won't be seeing them again for a while, after all. I recommend you stock up.

They proceed to buy a large amount, and I mess with the slot's jackpot chances a bit and give one to Gorth, but not Karios. Certainly *not* out of a bias against the in-your-face I'm-further-along-in-life-than-you stuff recently.

"Oh, the captain brought them. Lammis, Boxxo, pleased to meet you."

"Yeah. Welcome, both of you—person and machine both."

"Nice to meetcha!"

This group is like a big family, and while there does seem to be a rank system, most of them seem generally familiar with one another. The members of our expeditionary force include the captain, the vice captain, the archer girl who was there during the frog-fiend hunt, and two young men who look like twins and seem good-natured.

"Great, let's head out. Hurry up and get her ready!" Captain Kerioyl gives a kick to the cart wheel to rush the twins, reclining in the covered wagon. They move around to the coachman seats as the captain and vice captain climb aboard. "Lammis and Boxxo, you can get in, too."

"No, I'll run for now! It'll be good for my training. And I think if I put Boxxo in there, it'll be hard for the buar."

Well, we do have the weight of quite a few people. I might be a bigger burden than if everyone was on there at once.

"Great, then I'll get in instead," says Hulemy, who I thought had come to see us off, boarding the cart. Wait, what?!

"Huh? Hulemy, you're coming, too?"

"That's right. You're doing biological research on monsters—you'll want someone with a lot of knowledge on them. I got the request from Director Bear himself."

She was keeping quiet just to surprise us, wasn't she? Come to think of it, she never did seem very worried about us.

They may call themselves the Menagerie of Fools, but their skills are the real deal. They can be her bodyguard, so I think even Hulemy, with no combat abilities, should be fine, but there's no telling what could happen in an alternate world where monsters exist. I can protect her if I'm nearby, but I'll be mainly moving with Lammis, so she'll probably end up hiding in the cart.

An adventure... I was reborn into this world as a vending machine and would normally have just lived out my life as a metal box that simply sold things. I didn't think I'd be wandering the dungeon like this.

You never know what will happen in life—whether you're a person or a vending machine.

As I bump around on Lammis's back as she runs alongside the buar cart, matching its speed, I gaze with deep emotion at the settlement as it shrinks into the distance.

Along for the Ride

As I stare at the grassy fields and the clouds dotting the sky, she carries me…but I mustn't think about that too hard.

About three hours after leaving early this morning, we stop to take a quick break.

The giant buar seems to still have some energy in it, and Lammis, who was running alongside it, isn't showing any signs of tiredness, either. Once again, I'm in awe of her insane physical abilities.

A break didn't seem necessary to me, but it's apparently a bathroom break. There are more women than men in our group, so the place and timing for them to do their business must be the problem. They can't go number one wherever they want and be done with it like men.

The issue is a realistic one for women that you wouldn't have known from games. Wait, I think there was something suited for this very situation.

I scroll down to the bottom part of the features list and select it, pay the points, and acquire it. Then I immediately change into it.

I've already been placed to one side of the cart, but when they see my form change, the twins and the archer girl begin to gape. Have they never seen this before?

"Hey, Boxxo, are you going to show us a new feature…hmm? There's something attached to your side now."

As Hulemy says, I didn't change my body this time—instead, a new object appeared next to me. It looks like a thin, tall locker, exactly the same height as I am.

The bottom of it is a waste bin. The upper part has a fixed covering, and when removed, there's a folding chair, a cardboard box, and another long, thin cardboard box packed inside.

"What's this? If Boxxo chose now to make it, it must mean something."

"Welcome."

"For now, let's open it and take out what's inside. Is that okay?"

"Welcome."

Without fear, Hulemy begins to remove the contents. Lammis and the Menagerie of Fools watch her with bated breath.

"This is a folding chair. But why is there a hole where you sit down? It's strange to the touch, and inside it, strange-feeling paper? Can I open it?"

"Welcome."

"I'll just keep going, so if you don't want me to do something, tell me. Anyway, this paper is tough, and it looks like a bag."

"Hey, Hulemy, doesn't it look like that bag fits perfectly inside the hole in the chair?"

"Hmm... Oh, it's just right. Good job, Lammis. We also have this huge, thin box. I'll open this, too... There's a clear bag inside, and then inside that is... Whoa!"

Hulemy brings it out, and it pops out to three times its length. It's a fold-up tent, but the convenient kind where all you need to do is unfold it.

"Th-that's a surprise. Its shape is fixed in advance, and just a touch reverts it to its original form? It might be a magic item."

Despite her shock, her curiosity seems to win out, and after a wince, she manages to spread the tent out.

"An object like a tent the size for one person to fit inside. A chair with a hole in it and a bag... Hey, wait, is this a simple toilet?!" cries Hulemy, the eyes of all the women in the group lighting up.

Yes. This is a simple toilet for disaster sites, fixed to the sides of vending machines as a service for use during emergencies. In recent years, there was a serious toilet problem after a certain disaster occurred. As a free service, a vending machine manufacturer affixed boxes with simple toilets inside them to their machines.

There still weren't very many, but I encourage the kind of goodwill in creating something like this, so if I saw one, I always bought something at it.

"This small tent can be closed up, so nobody can see. And if you close the bag after using it, the odor won't escape, either."

"I-is that true?!" cries the vice captain, Filmina, in an unusually loud tone, pressing Hulemy, who had explained it.

"Y-yeah. I don't think there's much doubt about it. There's a scent coming from the thing at the bottom of the bag, which must be a deodorizer. Right, Boxxo?"

"Welcome."

"See?"

The women of the group, eyes alight, rush to be the first to use the simple toilet. Hulemy goes in first to test it, and when she comes out with satisfaction on her face, they form a line.

"Boxxo, this is something else. There's probably hunters out there who would *pay* for something like this."

The women's toilet situation here must be worse than I thought. This is a free disaster service, so I can't take your money.

Well, after that, the hunters who used the toilet all thanked me and bought a drink, so I guess that's fine.

"How do you like it? I'm the one who invited Boxxo, and now you get to use this handy little toilet. Go ahead—you can feel free to praise your captain some more!"

"This is Mr. Boxxo's talent, not your achievement, Captain," says Filmina flatly over her shoulder. The captain leaves, looking a bit sullen.

The simple toilet is a huge success, and after they use it, they dig a hole in the ground to bury the used bags in. I can also erase any products I've created at will, so in consideration for soil contamination, I destroy the bags—the waste will eventually degrade.

They fold the simple toilet set back up and place it on the cart. The disaster set, too, consumes points, so I'll have them carry it instead of erasing it. Once the expedition is over, though, I'll get it back from them.

"Let's have an early lunch while we're at it."

Now, here's where I really come in. I provide a wide assortment of products at half the price I offer them for in the settlement.

Normally, they would probably sell even if I set the prices to be a bit high, but the Menagerie of Fools promised a reward beforehand, so if I provide them this service, it should make a good advertisement for when Lammis does work as a hunter in the future.

"These hardened, fried grains are incredible!"

"Wait, really? This pasta is crazy rich in flavor, too."

The two twin hunters are being friendly, sharing their food as they eat. One of them has red hair, and the other has white hair. I decide to dub them the red-and-white twins. In fact, the others simply call them Red and White.

"Wow, I never thought I'd be able to eat such delicious food on an expedition. I'm so glad I came!"

The archer girl's hair is cut short enough to see the back of her neck; she looks like a man at first, but her voice is high-pitched, like a moe character in an anime.

Before her sits—or rather, sat—takoyaki, yakisoba, instant ramen, karaage, and a two-liter bottle of cola. Their contents are all empty now. Despite being so petite, she put it all away pretty easily. Even eating-contest champions would be surprised at her appetite.

"Shui's appetite is huge, as usual. Thanks to you, Mr. Boxxo, we don't have to worry about how much food we have left." Vice Captain Filmina sighs, twirling a lock of her wavy blue hair with a finger. With a big eater like her, they probably have food shortages not long into any extended expeditions.

"You mean we don't have to catch monsters and roast them this time?!"

"Oh, thank goodness… Thank goodness!"

The red-and-white twins hug, overjoyed. Have they been catching monsters to eat every time? The snake looked tasty, but the frog people? Come to think of it, when I first met Lammis, she was trying to catch a frog person for a meal.

The residents of this world must not have much resistance to eating monsters. When dining outdoors, the hunters generally have nothing

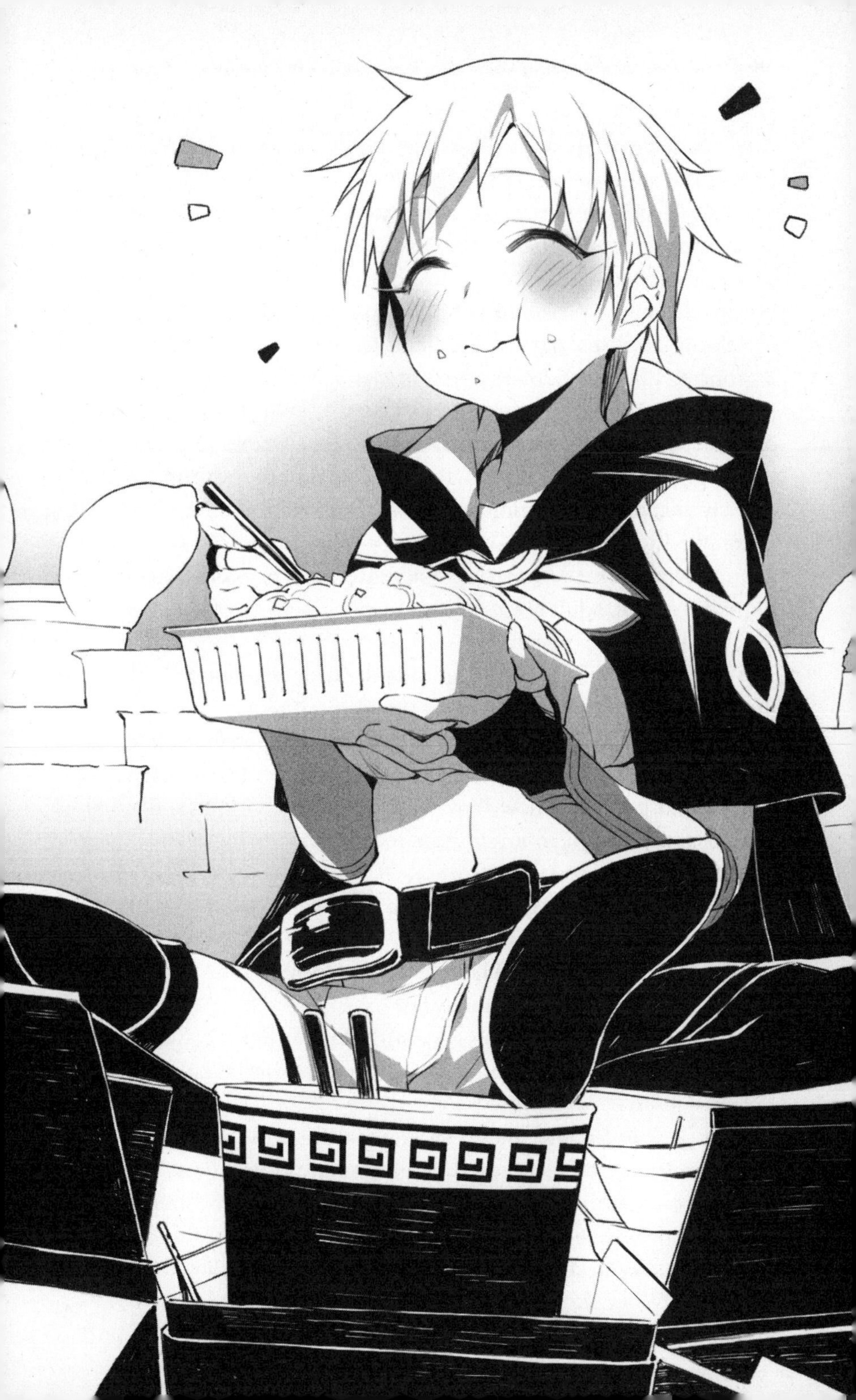

more than provisions and seasoned herbs, so I can understand their admiration for a vending machine's food.

Simple toilet or not, if I temporarily travel with teams of hunters and do business, it seems like I'll be able to make significant profits. Manpower is needed to carry my vending machine body, so it would probably also lower the possibility of harm coming to Lammis.

But if I'm thinking about safety, then it would be best to belong to a group of talented hunters like this Menagerie of Fools… Hmm. Worrying over it won't do me any good; Lammis is the one to decide that. I can't give her a single word of advice, but I'll be watching closely during this expedition to see exactly what kind of team they are.

My heartfelt resolution on the subject is all well and good, but there's nothing in particular to do at the moment. We began proceeding again after our break, but the occasional appearances of frog people and a smaller—well, adult-size—double serpent met with a volley of arrows and water magic from afar.

Apart from that, a throwing knife occasionally launches off the top of the cart's covering, where the captain is napping, sending a monster falling flat on its back, the knife hilt sticking out of its head like a horn.

They're something else. I see why the younger hunters aspire to be like them. I got to see how they fight during the king-frog-fiend affair, but observing them in a relaxed situation makes me want to sigh in admiration.

The enemies never get close, so for now, the twins and Lammis have no chance to battle.

"Boxxo, do you think I should do something, too?" asks Lammis. "Should I throw rocks or something?"

Projectile weapons? She's generally clumsy, but it could work with that excessive Might of hers. Do I have anything suitable for her to throw?

If I got her to wrap me in chains and fling me around, I'd expect some significant attack power, but Lammis would never do that.

Hmm—a throwing weapon. What about those nostalgic cans of soda from last time? Those have enough weight and hardness to them, so they should be strong. They fit your hand, too, so they must be easy to throw.

I've got nothing to lose by testing it. I stock the soda cans and drop one.

She's carrying me facing forward right now, so despite the awkward pose, she can locate my compartment by reaching around. As she walks, she manages to pull it out.

"Hmm? This is the bubbly juice, right? Wait, there's something different inside this one. It's hard."

"Maybe he's telling you to throw it," pipes in Hulemy, her head poking out of the cart.

It seems to click, and Lammis pounds her palm with a fist, nodding in understanding. Perfect timing, too—a frog human appeared in front of us, so she takes the can of juice in her hand, swings it around, and hurls it.

The can flies in a completely different direction, disappearing into some weeds. The frog person looks at her with a dubious shrug.

"Ugh, how frustrating!"

Her Might must still be too much for it. She can throw things, but as for her precision—well, I'm sure you can guess. She might as well throw me instead. I get the feeling that would be more accurate.

Anyway, after that, the frog person quite quickly finds the crown of its head pierced with an arrow and falls over. It doesn't look like Lammis will get a turn for a while.

Crocodiles and How to
Deal with Them

The buar cart comes to a stop in a depression on a rocky hill as the man sleeping on top of the cart's covering gives a full stretch and lets out big yawn. "We're in their territory now," he says sleepily, "so look sharp."

"Then why don't you come down from there as well, Captain?"

"Want to spear him from underneath?"

I think that's a good idea. Nice suggestion, red-and-white twins.

Two days have passed since leaving the settlement; we're on our third day now. We seemed to enter crocodile-fiend territory as a star, which I believe is the sun, climbed to its apex overhead.

"Captain, please, get down already. We're here for reconnaissance and investigation."

"All right, all right. Sheesh. You're so quick to anger, Vice Captain."

Holding his hat with his right hand so it doesn't fly off, Captain Kerioyl jumps down. Frustratingly, the movement is fluid, and I accidentally think to myself that it looked a little cool.

"Red, White, you two are on reconnaissance, then."

"Will do."

"Aye, aye, sir!"

Are they usually on scouting duty? Looking at them, they seem like the characters in charge of hyping up the mood, the kind you usually see at least one of in any real-life friend group. The sort you'd expect to be gung ho about everything.

They're not unattractive, but their tones are too silly, and their personalities are too easygoing for Lammis or Hulemy to fall for either of them, even by mistake.

Red uses a short spear as his weapon, and White uses a short sword. Their armor consists of things that look like button-down shirts made from thick fabric, their coloring a well-worn brown. They must get a lot of use out of them.

Whoa, their expressions just vanished. Their eyes sharpen, and the air around them changes in an instant. If they were always like that, they might actually be popular.

The two crouch and disappear into the tall grasses. Since this is a marshland, simply walking might be heard, but they're *running* without making a sound. Despite their appearances, they seem quite talented.

"Great, let's put our feet up until they get back. Boxxo, you got any good sweets in there?"

"I'll have some sweet tea."

"Welcome."

Both the captain and vice captain have moved into relaxation mode. Neither displays a hint of worry. The other member, the girl with the short hair, simply adjusts her bow, not paying any mind to the pair that went off to scout. They must be well trusted.

Lammis leans up against my back to take a comfortable nap. Hulemy seems to have taken an interest in how cans work. Without taking a sip of hers, she fiddles with it, jotting things down in a small notepad.

It's all so defenseless, considering crocodile fiends are on the prowl in this region, but their skills are first-rate. Maybe there's no need for me to be on my guard. But I won't slip up and make the same mistake again.

When the sun sets over halfway, the Menagerie of Fools begins to make camp. Lammis tries to help as well, but they politely refuse. She's broken equipment and items with her excessive Might in the past, so they're probably being wary of that.

She sits next to me, looking a little alienated, so I give her a warm milk tea as a present.

Don't worry about it so much, Lammis. Just take it easy. Look at Hulemy—scratching at her exposed, bloated tummy, snoring away... Okay, maybe you don't need to learn from her.

"We're back."

"All finished!"

Whoa, that scared me. I didn't notice the red-and-white twins suddenly standing next to me. I don't know whether a vending machine can sense presences, but I didn't even notice one bit.

"Captain, we've taken a look around."

"Nice work," says Kerioyl. "Dinner's soon, so give me your report."

"Aye, aye, sir. Um, it was about two hours northeast from here, right, Red?"

"About that, White. There's a small marsh there, with about thirty of them splashing around in it."

They call each other Red and White? Their explanation was half-hearted, too. Are things going to be all right? I'm a little worried.

"Thirty, eh? How big a bask is that?" asks the captain, looking over to Hulemy, who has woken up and is now examining a plastic bottle's material again.

"Hmm. They say a bask can be anywhere from ten to fifty at most. Thirty is a middle-size one. How big were the individuals?"

"Well, they were about the same height as us standing up, right, White?"

"Yeah, Red. About that height."

A little shorter than I am, then. Pretty big specimens. Considering what the frog people look like, I imagine crocodiles standing up straight on two legs, with their arms and legs the same length as usual, which probably makes them slow-moving.

"That's punier than normal. Normally, they're about five feet. The frogs increased in number and made their own group, so maybe the crocodiles have been out of food since they can't attack... Well actually, if there's thirty, they could take on close to a hundred."

By simple math, that means the crocodile people have three times the strength of frog people. Their skin is hard as armor, too, and their tails and giant mouths are fine weapons. I suppose it's not strange for there to be such a power differential.

"We're not experts on this stratum, so maybe I'm talking out of my butt. But the crocodile fiends are the most violent of the Three Factions here, right? If there were more frog friends, why didn't they go and have themselves a feast?"

"Normally, you'd think that. But there was a king frog fiend there this time. We don't know the conditions for a king to appear, and its crazy power is one thing, but the issue is that it can unify armies of frogs. Even the smaller armies and rogue ones will gather together."

"And that meant the crocodile fiends had to be careful," said Kerioyl. "That giant double serpent that attacked the settlement was out of the ordinary, too."

Ah, I've been wondering about that. I've heard the double-serpent fiends generally move alone, and they're about five feet in size.

"The more a double-serpent fiend eats, the more times it molts, getting bigger every time. But their meat is very tasty, and their materials sell for a high price, so a lot of hunters go after them. If any are wandering around alone, they make a perfect target."

Frog fiends are targeted by crocodile fiends and double-serpent fiends.

Double serpents are targeted by hunters.

And the crocodile fiends...are left alone?

"Anyway, yeah. Their food source, the frog fiends, rallied under a king, the double serpents devoured all that remained—not that there was much to begin with—to get giant, making them hard to deal with. Probably means the crocodiles are weakened now due to food shortages."

"I see," says Kerioyl. "We don't have to do anything about them, then, do we?"

"Captain, crocodile fiends are carnivorous. With a lack of a food supply, what do you think they'll attack to sate their hunger?"

"Well, us humans, I guess. Then we should wipe them all out?"

What is going on with the ecosystem on this stratum? If they wipe out all the monsters, will they just disappear from the stratum? Or do they bubble forth from some mysterious power in the dungeon?

I'm sure if I asked Hulemy, she'd be more than happy to explain, but I have no way to bring up the topic.

"I don't believe there would be an issue were we to eliminate a bask close to the settlement."

Unusually, Vice Captain Filmina is in agreement.

Come to think of it, doesn't it take three weeks of walking to get from one end of the Clearflow Lake stratum to the other? I understand what she means—wiping out a bask two or three days out shouldn't cause a problem.

"Anyway, what are we doing? The request was to gather information on their basks. We don't have to beat them—we'll get a reward anyway."

"But we can sell materials scavenged from them for high prices. I believe we have the option of felling several of the weakened ones ourselves. Those materials are valuable."

What's this? I've never seen Vice Captain Filmina raring for battle before. Wait, is the Menagerie of Fools in a financial crisis?

"She really changes when it comes to money."

"She's normally so calm and collected, too."

"Last time, she got angry at me and said it was because I eat too much."

The members huddle around and trade hushed remarks.

It's possible she's just a miser… But I guess under such a haphazard captain, one would naturally become strict with money management. From the looks of things, they do seem to be having a hard time.

"If we wanted to exterminate them, how would we do it?" asks Lammis. "Wait until night and attack, I guess?"

"You'd better not," says Hulemy. "Crocodile fiends are nocturnal. They get more violent at night."

"Huh, I see."

Huh, I see. Ack, I said the same thing as Lammis. Hulemy really does know a lot.

Crocodilian ecology, huh? This one time, when I went to a zoo to see its animal-feed vending machines, I took a peek at the crocodile corner, and something was written there.

What do crocodiles eat again…? I remember seeing people feeding them fish and chicken. The vending machines didn't carry raw food. Fish…paste products…*chikuwa* fish cakes— No, that wouldn't work.

As for other characteristics... Oh, they mentioned how the frog people are weak with the winter, so maybe the cold affects the crocodile people, too. Crocodiles are cold-blooded, so it's possible.

In the first place, the entire point was to get recon on the crocodile people before they entered their active season. We're on the cusp of spring now, with the temperature on the rise. Coldness... Could I do *that*, maybe?

"Well, let's all get a good rest tonight, then, and move out tomorrow morning," says Kerioyl. "We'll take care of any of them that stray from the bask!"

"I agree. We shall move tomorrow, and for now, we will make dinner. Red and White, please keep watch."

"What? But we just came back from our reconnaissance."

"You're a tyrant! I demand better working conditions!"

"All right, all right. I'll help, too, so let's get going."

As the twins complain of discontent, the archer girl goes between them, takes their arms, and drags them away.

After they finish the meal they made with the ingredients I provided, Lammis and Hulemy request to go on watch, so I decide to go with them. I'll turn off my vending machine light for now.

"Tomorrow's the battle, eh? You won't be needing me, then. Lammis, Boxxo, don't do anything crazy. It's highly likely they'll be real violent, thanks to the food shortage. If things get bad, Boxxo, protect her with your Force Field."

"Welcome."

"I'll be counting on you, Boxxo!"

Roger that. Protection is my specialty. I have quite a few points to spare, so I'll put my heart and soul into it if it comes to it.

"I still wish I could help, though."

Oh, right. I wonder if Hulemy would be able to guess the trick I thought of earlier. Let's give it a try.

"If the crocodile fiends have any weakness, it's— Whoa, what's up, Boxxo? You changed shape again."

My form becomes slimmer than normal, with most of my body becoming white and the word ICE appearing on the top part. The compartment is fairly large—there's easily enough space to put a bucket in there.

"What does this one sell? Boxxo wouldn't change forms without a reason."

You got it, Lammis. If you look inside, you'll realize what I'm selling right away.

I rev up my vending machine engines and drop some ice cubes into my compartment. This is an ice vending machine, the kind in supermarkets and fish markets.

"Whoa, is this ice? I bet this would sell really well in the summer."

"*Fwah*, it's cold. But what do you want to do with this ice?"

"Based on what we were talking about earlier, you want to use this ice to help exterminate the crocodile fiends?"

"Are we going to throw them?!"

That idea is very much like Lammis, but that's "Too bad."

"Ice, crocodile fiends, ecology—there's only one answer. Boxxo, can you put out cartfuls of this ice, by chance?"

"Welcome."

"I see how it is. This could get interesting."

"Hey, come on, tell me so I can understand, too!"

Oh, Lammis can't keep up, and now she's puffing out her cheeks and sulking.

I'll let Hulemy explain in detail. She won't listen to me once she gets mad at something, after all… It's in your hands now. I'll do my best as a lookout in your stead.

As I watch over Hulemy trying to soothe and humor Lammis, I use my Omnidirectional Vision to its fullest, keeping watch alone until she's out of her bad mood.

When Hulemy explains the tactic the next day to the Menagerie of Fools, they seem like they're all for it and decide to help. The red-and-white twins guide us to a stream that flows into the lake, and they set me down next to it. Then I begin pouring ice into it.

The stream isn't even a foot wide, so it doesn't have much water, but the ice floats up to its surface perfectly and flows toward the lake.

Time to give it everything I've got. Well, I have huge doubts as to how much this ice will actually lower the temperature, but the marsh isn't that large. It's still very early spring, so the water is cold; the ice should have trouble melting. Marshes serving as crocodile-fiend habitats are apparently shallow, so it should decrease the water temperature by some degree... I hope.

The crocodile fiends are the toughest to handle when they're in the water, so if the temperature falls to a point where they decide to get out of the marsh, that'll be a huge help, according to them. Which means it's time to dump truckloads of ice in.

The cubes continue to clatter out and into the stream. The point conversion for ice is pretty cheap, so I can keep dumping it for about an hour and not hurt much.

It would be a godsend if their body temperature fell at all and their movements dulled. This is a cheap cost if it means making Lammis's fight easier.

Crocodile Hunting

"Captain, the crocodile fiends have gone up to the banks. They were shivering like they were cold. They were falling asleep, too."

When Red, who was scouting out the marsh, returns, he gives his report on the situation.

Captain Kerioyl, reclining atop a large boulder, says "Good work" and waves a hand. "Sounds good to me, but even if they can't move, the others will react if we attack. Vice Captain, can you block their sight with mist magic?"

"It isn't impossible, but covering the entire marsh in mist has its limits."

Mist magic? Cool. There's a certain elegance to mist hovering over a marsh. I would very much like to see that, but I guess the area she'd need to cover is too big. If we want to create mist on the marsh, then I wonder if this will help.

"So what do we do?" muses Captain Kerioyl. "Split them up and… What are you doing, Boxxo?"

Upon seeing me change forms, the captain's hat slides down. This time, I change into a vending machine with a silvery, cylindrical body and a clear door attached at right about the middle.

I open the door and let a white chunk of matter fall from a silver tube inside me. It sits there, white steam billowing from it.

"Wait, what's this?" says the captain, seeming interested and jumping off the boulder to get a closer peek at the white lump. "It's too cloudy to be ice. Is it like a hardened chunk of snow?"

He moves to touch it with a finger, at which point I drop another one and say, "Too bad."

"Captain, I think maybe Boxxo is saying you shouldn't touch it," suggests Lammis.

"It might be dangerous to touch bare-handed," adds Hulemy.

"Welcome." They're both right. But actions speak louder than words—I drop more of the white matter, and it overflows from my compartment and falls into the stream. As soon as it touches the water, it begins to emit clouds of vapor.

"Whoa, what's that?!" cries the captain. "It spouted mist!" He jumps behind me, staring at the white matter floating down the stream, creating white smoke—dry ice. That was a funny reaction, Captain.

I think everyone's tested at least once how dry ice creates white smoke when you put it in water. I wasn't sure if this could be a substitute for mist. What do they think?

"Mr. Boxxo, this is incredible!" says the vice captain. "If we combine this with my mist magic, we might be able to cover the entire marsh with it."

"That's really something, Boxxo. I knew it was a good idea to bring you along."

"Yes, he's more useful than you are, Captain."

"Guh!" The vice captain Filmina's cold words cause the captain to clutch his chest and stagger backward.

"We should just make Boxxo the captain."

"That's a good idea, White," says Red. "The name Menagerie of Fools is pretty dumb, too. We could change it to something cute like the Boxxo Brigade."

"H-how could you?" stammers the captain, fighting against the twins' follow-up attack. "I thought long and hard about this perfect, tasteful name, and that's what you thought about it this whole time?"

"I mean, fools? A menagerie?" pipes in the archer girl, adding her finishing blow. "Boxxo Brigade sounds cute. I bet it will be popular with girls. If Mr. Boxxo is our captain, we can have as much to eat as we want! I like the idea a lot!"

"Aaarrrggghhh!" The captain curls up and stomps on the ground. How sad.

"All right, all right, let's leave the fooling around at that," says the vice captain. "Don't lose your nerve now, Captain. Your instructions, please."

"Ugh. Just take them down however you want. Your useless captain will have some sweet tea and watch from a distance so he doesn't get in your way."

Ah, he's kicking stones by the stream, obviously sulking. What are you, five?

Of course, his whining doesn't work, and the other members drag him away.

"Um, I'm going to go, too," says Lammis. "You have to stay here and keep putting that into the stream, right? Will you stay behind here with Hulemy?"

"Welcome."

"Sure. Take care out there. If it gets dangerous, come back right away."

"Yup. I'll be back soon!"

I can't move from here, thanks to my job dropping the dry ice, but not being able to go with her makes me uneasy. They're only going to hunt a group of weakened enemies, so I don't think there's much chance anything will happen to them, but it makes me worry when she's not at my back.

"Hey, don't worry. The Menagerie of Fools is a very skilled team of hunters. They know when to pull out. If things get dangerous, they'll come back, I'm telling you." Hulemy hits me a few times, apparently trying to be considerate.

I'll trust that they'll be all right. I have to focus on my work. As I drop the dry ice into the stream, all I can do is watch silently as they begin to disappear into the mist filling the area.

"You seem bored, Boxxo."

"Welcome."

When things are like this, there's nothing for the noncombatants to do. I'm still setting dry ice afloat in the stream, but I start to feel sorry when I consider the fact that I have no way to fight after being reborn in another world.

"Then, let's talk about stuff to pass the time."

"Welcome."

"For this scouting mission, you remember how I said the director himself came to request my aid, right? He said he wanted me to investigate the state of the Clearflow Lake stratum, since odd things have been happening lately. And that if the crocodile fiends on this mission looked strange, too, we'd have to take extra precautions."

A frog king and an enormous snake. Even a native of a different world can tell something is off here. If something is up with the crocodile fiends as well, I would naturally assume something is wrong.

"You may not know this, Boxxo, but on each stratum, there's something called a stratum lord. You open up the next stratum by defeating the stratum lord. Once you beat one, they almost never come back. But in rare cases, they will revive. We still don't know the conditions, but sometimes it takes years or even decades."

A stratum lord? That must be the boss character at the end of every stratum, like in dungeon crawler games. Normally, they'll be blocking the stairway that leads down to the next floor, or waiting for you in front of a door.

"So apparently, the director thinks the disturbances may indicate the stratum lord's revival. I've told the Menagerie of Fools as much, too. If they sense things are bad, I'm sure they'll retreat without a second thought. Oh, and if you beat a stratum lord, the rumor is that you get an amazing treasure. I'm sure it's made-up, though."

Our scouting mission was that important? I wonder what kind of monster the stratum lord here is. Maybe a mixture of frog, crocodile, and snake—like a chimera?

Obviously, it's going to have to be huge. It might be fifteen feet tall. If I could watch from a safe distance, I'd want to see it in action.

If the stratum lord really has revived, it might be a good idea to consider moving to a different stratum, or to the surface. Well, I'll have to leave that decision to Lammis and Hulemy.

The stratum lord's presence worries me, but right now I'm more anxious about Lammis's safety—or rather, whether or not she'll mess something up.

"Besides, it's not like we'd attract the stratum lord from the very beginning or anything."

Hulemy, we call that a *flag* where I come from. You have to keep ill-omened thoughts like that to yourself, or they'll end up happening for real.

If I could talk, I'd give her a witty retort, but a moment later those thoughts vanish.

"What's this rumbling?"

I can feel slight vibrations from the part of me touching the ground. I have a bad feeling about this, but when I look toward the sound's source—I see a buar cart charging full speed toward us. The cart's covering is gone, exposing those riding it.

The red- and white-haired twins are in the front seats. Behind them is the captain, wearing a tense expression. Behind him are the archer girl, Shui, and the vice captain, Filmina, facing backward, launching arrows and magic.

Lammis—where's Lammis?! I can't seem to find her anywh— There she is!

She's leaning back against the cart's railing, eyes closed, not moving. I-is she okay?!

"Hey, hey, hey, you've got to be kidding me! Damn, it's a firefight. Did the stratum lord show up?!"

"The stratum lord?!" I would have said, if I had a voice.

Hulemy stares dumbfounded, past the buar cart, at the small mountain following from behind.

No, I haven't gone crazy. An object that can only be described as a small mountain is chasing them from behind. The buar cart looks like a miniature figurine—the thing is so large, it's throwing off my sense of perspective. On the whole, it looks like a giant crocodile. You know, save for its eight legs and four eyes. One of those feet is big enough to cover the buar cart entirely. I knew it would be giant, but this is ridiculous. Can people even kill something like that?!

It's got eight legs, so the vibrations continue. I feel my vending machine body almost hop into the air.

"Ahhh, shit!" curses Hulemy bitterly. "It's even causing a stratum split, isn't it?!"

I follow her gaze and see fissures running along the ground, and then I catch a glimpse of light flowing out of them. Is that the stratum split?

I don't really get it, but I do understand this is an extreme emergency.

Wh-what do I do? The buar cart is rushing full speed toward us. They might be able to pick up Hulemy, but will they have time to get me on board? ...Not a chance.

Then there's only one thing to do!

"Lammis is only unconscious!" shouts the captain. "Hulemy, give me your hand! Grab onto mine!"

"What about Boxxo? Are we just gonna leave him here?!"

"Welcome," I answer to her question to the captain.

Hulemy turns a baffled look on me. I activate Force Field to get her away from me.

"Boxxo, what are you doing?!"

"Sorry, Boxxo. We'll come back for you, I swear it!" apologizes the captain, lowering his head as they run straight by me and he sweeps Hulemy up, his entire upper body leaning out of the cart.

"Let me go, dammit! Boxxo! *Boxxooooooo!*"

"Please come again."

They run farther away behind me, and after a farewell, I stare straight ahead.

Lammis being out cold might actually be a good thing. She would have jumped off the cart and tried to stay with me otherwise.

I know exactly what I have to do here. I may not be able to fight as a vending machine, but I can at least be a decoy! Time for a form change!

My body grows straight upward, reaching a height of ten feet. The colors on it change into something much flashier, and my products turn into only soda. This vending machine is a giant one from a certain theme park, a crazy piece of equipment where you have to stand on someone else's shoulders to even buy anything.

The approaching giant eight-legged crocodile appears to be going after the buar cart, but the sudden appearance of a giant, conspicuous object in front of it seems to draw its attention.

Its four eyes all lock onto me. To grab its attention even more, I raise my volume to maximum.

"Welcome. Welcome. Welcome. Welcome."

The eight-legged crocodile reacts to my loud, resounding voice. Its bloodthirsty gaze pierces my metal body. Whoa, that's terrifying! What'll you do if my products freeze?

As it gets closer, my view begins to fill with the eight-legged crocodile's skin color. It's like a dirty green on black, and soon the color is the only thing I can see. The mud peculiar to marshlands erupts out of the ground—it'll reach me in only a few seconds at this rate.

I gambled on my Force Field being able to withstand the rubble as it collapses, but if any get through, my chronicle will end. I decide to raise my durability from one hundred to two hundred and my toughness from thirty to fifty.

That consumes ten thousand and nine thousand points respectively, but that might as well be a drop in the bucket.

As I watch the astoundingly large feet stomp toward me, a feeling close to resignation begins to set in—and suddenly, I'm hurtling backward with no respect for gravity.

[Points decreased by 1,000.]

Ahhhh! This feeling like my body is being pulled backward—did that thing kick me away? Vending machines really can fly... No, now isn't the time for jokes!

I fly dozens of yards away, crash into a boulder, and come to a stop. I didn't take any damage, thanks to my Force Field, but my points decreased by a thousand for some reason. Didn't Force Field take one point per second? I didn't get any message like that when I stopped the rubble with it.

Maybe I can only maintain the Force Field by spending a lot of points if I take an attack that has a higher power than it can handle.

The Force Field is denting the boulder. If I had taken that blow defenseless, I'd have been wiped out of existence.

And now I have an even bigger reason not to let it chase after Lammis and the others.

The Fighting Vending Machine

To buy time, I might manage by just getting knocked around by the monster and enduring with Force Field, but if it heads for the settlement afterward, I'm not sure even the Hunters Association's sturdy fortress could hold out.

At the very least, they won't be able to save everyone in the settlement like they did last time.

The inn's mistress and Munami have done so much for me; the gatekeepers Karios and Gorth are my number-one customers; the group of three that comes every morning—no, four, now that their granddaughter has been with them recently; Shirley buys all the contraceptives I can dispense; the blond-haired young lady, the people in black, the two money changers, and all my other customers are in that settlement.

A vending machine's presence is like proof of peace and public order.

And that means there's no problem at all with me, a vending machine, protecting those in the settlement!

The eight-legged crocodile, seemingly aggravated by its fruitless attempts to break my body despite sending me flying several times, charges toward my position even faster than before.

Even if I defend against it, it'll knock me miles away. I might lose sight of it, and it could even lose interest in the big white vending machine. If that happens, it would expose the fleeing Lammis and the others to danger. Then how about this?!

I change into a homemade bento vending machine I found locally once. Then I dump a pile of fried-food bento boxes into my compartment. My rough handling of them causes the food to spill from their boxes, sending the scent of fried food—warmed by my heat retention—drifting into the air nearby.

I don't know whether crocodiles have a good sense of smell, but one that giant must be starving all the time. And it should be feeling mad, since no matter how many times it attacks, it can't destroy me.

If there was something exuding a delicious scent before its eyes right now, what would it do?

The answer comes from the crocodile's mouth—and the lines of sharp teeth inside it.

No sooner do I feel my body shake left and right than I suddenly begin to fall straight up. It looks like there are long dark-red tubes running around me. This must be its esophagus.

Force Field is protecting me even in this situation. I continue to hurtle down the beast's gullet, then hear the sound of something dropping into liquid. After I rise to the surface of the sticky fluid, I look around. Several rocks and trees with melted leaves are floating around as well.

Ah, I must be in its stomach.

[Points decreased by 10. Points decreased by 10.]

The stomach acid begins to deplete my points incredibly quickly. It looks like I won't be able to relax in this situation. If this is its stomach—then I'll go ahead and start harassing it!

Using my Boxed-Item Support feature, I switch my products. I change them into cleaning detergent found at a coin laundry, start pouring them into my compartment, then use Force Field's ability to launch them outside the barrier.

The detergent flies from my compartment outside my Force Field, bubbling and sinking into the stomach acid.

You'll be writhing in intense pain in a second. It's my treat—time for the stomach cleaning of a lifetime!

As one container of detergent sinks after another, the stomach acid begins to ripple. I can tell firsthand that the eight-legged crocodile is squirming in agony. It seems to be working very well.

But it probably won't die from just this. No matter how I think about it, diarrhea and nausea is as far as this will go. Which means it's time to change into an older body that I just acquired.

Attached to my patented retro-silver rectangular body is a lever you can crank manually. The bottom part has orange tubes extending from it, connecting to an old cooking stove.

This is a gas vending machine—one that I saw every once in a blue moon in old *ryokan* inns, hospitals, and dormitories. One hundred yen gives you a few minutes' worth of usage time. I initially thought it was a convenient feature for cooking outdoors, but I didn't think I'd be able to sell my vending machine products, so it's one of those features I haven't used.

I changed into a gas vending machine for one purpose: to spout gas outside my Force Field. I'll fill the creature's stomach to the brim with gas.

It's often said you'll get gas bubbles in your stomach when you eat too much, but this time, actual gas is spreading through. As I continue to release the gas, the stomach acid begins to churn around. My body rides the flow, the whirlpool steadily sucking me toward the center.

Does it plan to expel me from its body? I'll have to decide things before I get to its intestines. I don't know whether this is enough gas or if my Force Field will hold out—I need to try it to know for sure. It's worth a shot! I have faith!

…The issue is the fire. I figured I could just light the stove, but I don't have a way to turn the crank. I can manipulate my vending machine body to a certain extent, but the cooking stove seems like an external, optional part, and no matter how strongly I try, I can't control it.

This isn't what I expected. Crap—I'll be sucked in soon. Fire, fireworks, anything!

Wait, would *that* work?

I change into a vending machine that heats up frozen foods, then try refilling my canned products *inside* my internal microwave. I imagine replenishing my stock the same way I always do—but can I consciously send one of them into that microwave?

This vending machine is my body. I've been with it for months already. Please, at least give me this!

With a clattering that echoes through my body, I feel a single can appear.

Yes! I think I've got the hang of it, so I drop a towel and a newspaper into there, too.

This is the forbidden secret ceremony of heating up an aluminum can in the microwave! Don't try this at home, kids!

Frightened by the strange noises I start to hear from inside me, I feel the can launching sparks. I don't have sensations, but I seem to be able to understand what's happening in my body.

Oh, the flame lit.

[10 damage. Durability decreased by 10.]

Internal damage really hurts. But now everything is ready.

I drop the canned beverage and the towel, which is beginning to burn, along with the newspaper. And then I allow them to pass through my Force Field!

Out of my compartment flies the burning towel and newspaper-covered canned beverage. It looks as though I just shot a ball of fire.

The fireball is flung outside my Force Field, and as soon as it does, it makes contact with the gas filling the stomach—and causes a huge explosion.

"Please come again."

[Points decreased by 1,000.]

I can see something dark red scatter in front of me, but my vision is spinning like a top, so I have no idea what's actually happening.

Ohhh, I think I'm going to be sick! If its stomach exploded, it must be in unimaginable pain right now. Even this eight-legged crocodile, the stratum lord, will eventually breathe its last…right?!

All around me are walls of meat—dark-red, glossy, fleshy meat. The creature seems to be raging as usual, shaking its body intensely. If I had a physical body, I might have thrown up.

I don't know how much time passes, but at last, the shaking begins to die down. Did the eight-legged crocodile expire? If it did, the problem is how I get out of here.

[Points decreased by 1. Points decreased by 1.]

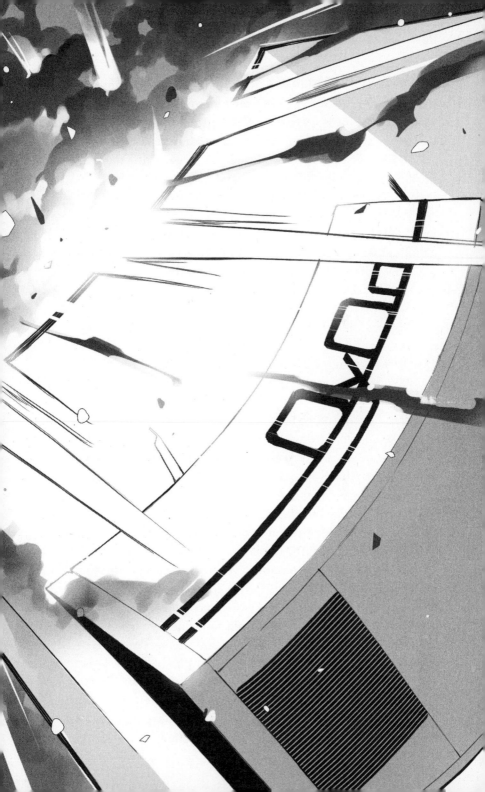

Ah yes, I know, I know. I still have my Force Field up, so my points are still going down. I've raised my toughness, and I think I'll be able to withstand the pressure from its flesh, but risking it still takes courage. If I go down to hardly any points, though, I'll have to turn it off anyway.

If that killed the monster, I can't ask for anything more. I used up a great number of the points I'd saved up, but I'm alive, and that's all that matters. Or *operational*, rather, since I'm a vending machine.

I must say, I've outdone myself this time. I did so well anyone would forgive me for tooting my own horn. Even vending machines can pull out all the stops when they need to. I think I feel a bit more confident now.

Now I'll·have to wait until Lammis and the others, having gotten away, come back—or until they return to the settlement and put together a hunting party. Also, I'm really glad I don't have a sense of smell.

At the earliest, half a day—and at the longest, weeks. I'm a vending machine, so staying in one place for a long time is part of the job. I'll just have to think about what new products to store— Eh?

Wait, the masses of meat filling my view disappeared. I can see the sky and the ground.

Wait, I'm outside, right? The creature's whole body is just gone. What the heck? I don't know what's happening, so I'll keep Force Field active.

I'm near the marsh we were at earlier. Fissures line the ground, golden light pouring from them. That must be the stratum split phenomenon Hulemy mentioned.

Then I must be outside, right? I look around; long, white connected things are positioned in such a way as to cover me up. This looks like… the eight-legged crocodile's skeleton.

Did its flesh disappear and leave only its bones? Is this how it works when you beat a stratum lord? The light from the fissures illuminates the crocodile's skeleton, giving it an almost mystical appearance.

That's a relief, I guess, but could someone help me up? I'm lying on my side right now, and it's a little uncomfortable. This kind of situation is a stark reminder of how inconvenient my body can be; I can't get back up by myself. Vending machines are supposed to stay standing.

Wait. I didn't realize this because of how bright the light from the fissures is, but there's a golden coin on the ground in front of me. This isn't a normal gold coin, is it? The decoration, as far as I can see, is completely different. Something is engraved in intense detail on it—an eight-legged crocodile.

In game terms, this might be the boss drop. You have to kill the boss to get this item, so it must be worth a lot, but I don't have any arms or legs, so I can't get it!

It's inside my Force Field, so I have to make sure nobody steals it. Hulemy probably knows more about this. I won't give it to anyone until then.

Anyway, I'm out of the belly of the beast, so all there is to be done is laze around and wait for someone to get here.

Hmm. It sort of feels like the ground is still shaking a little, and I can almost hear a creaking sound. It must be my imagination.

Hmmmm. The cracks in the ground run all over, kind of like netting, and the light from them is filling my vision with gold. I'm sure my eyes are just playing tricks on me.

Hmmmmmmm. I must be imagining this slow, sinking feeling—wait, it's caving in!

Huh? Did the foundation loosen after the commotion? Or is a stratum split just that—the stratum splitting apart?! W-wait a second. If that's right, when the ground splits, what happens then? W-will I fall?

This is fairly, no—*really* bad. No two ways about it. Wait, I remember feeling this once before.

Hey, someone! Isn't anyone with Might here?!

Isn't there a customer with Might who can easily pick up a vending machine around here?!

"Welcome. Welcome. Welcome," I repeat, but my words echo fruitlessly in the empty marshland.

I can really feel my gratitude toward Lammis now. I was on my high horse after beating such a strong enemy, but a vending machine is still just a vending machine. I can't do anything alone.

Oh.

The ground supporting me gives way, and I flip over as I begin to fall.

And in this back-to-the-wall situation, all I can think of is Lammis's crying face.

Rapid Descent

The earth cracks and collapses.

I'm currently descending rapidly along with earth and sand. When I look up, I can see an earthen ceiling and a big hole in it. The hole isn't that big, so while I fall, the eight-legged crocodile's bones avoid falling, the skeleton a covering over the hole.

And when I look down, there are clouds. I have my Force Field up, so I don't feel the wind force...but I can tell I'm falling incredibly fast!

Whaaat?! Going through the ground into the sky is right out of a fantasy novel!

Ahhh, I'm so high up I can't see the ground! Ahhh, oh, c-calm down!

First, I have to do something about my current situation. To do that, I need to understand it!

My location: the clouds!

My situation: falling!

The result: crashing and shattering!

It's over... No, I won't give up so easily. There's still time before I crash into the ground. Use your head. Think of a way out of this do-or-die situation.

All I can do is change my features. If I put my vending machine abilities to full use, can I manage somehow, some way?

If I'm descending, then I just need to slow my descent. What vending machine fits the bill? Oh, that!

I go into my list of features and choose Balloon Vending Machine, then change my body accordingly.

These used to be placed on supermarket roofs and in amusement parks a lot, but recently, they've become an old rarity you can only find at arcades and the like.

My body is mainly yellow and has a glass window, with lines of uninflated balloons beyond it. A buyer picks the color they want, and when they insert coins, the machine inflates it automatically for them.

Wait, now isn't the time for explanations! The color doesn't matter; I have to produce a lot of them.

I set up a balloon, and gas flows into it. A steadily expanding red balloon... No, this is taking far too much time. Can't I make them any more quickly? Can I increase the speed... Wait, if I raise my speed in my stats, won't that increase the inflation speed?!

Nothing to lose. No time. Let's try.

[Spend 10,000 points to raise speed by 10?]

Yeah, do it!

I feel the sensation of something entering me. And the balloon inflation speed... Oh! It's clearly faster now. It's over twice as fast as before. What if I increase it more?

[Spend 20,000 points to raise speed by 10?]

That's an awful markup, isn't it? Crap. Stupid points, taking advantage of me like this. Nothing good comes without sacrifice. Let's boost it another ten.

As though I'm watching a video on fast-forward, balloons inflate from start to finish in under two seconds. The inflated balloons stop inside my Force Field, packing the inside full.

Below me, I've gotten through the clouds, and I can see the ground... But what's that? A giant, complicated maze? Come to think of it, Hulemy said something about the strata before. If I recall, the stratum below Clearflow Lake was a maze or something.

Wait, now isn't the time to look fondly on the past. The labyrinth grows steadily, showing me a clear picture of its entirety. After all, my descent speed really hasn't changed much.

A few dozen balloons aren't going to support a vending machine weighing hundreds of pounds. I remember watching a variety show where it took over two thousand balloons just to make one adult float. I didn't think from the start that balloons could do anything for me.

The labyrinth walls are thick, and I've gotten close enough to the ground to realize how immensely tall they are. I seriously have no time left. Well then!

My choice here—I change forms into a cardboard vending machine!

Allow me to explain! A cardboard vending machine is a handmade vending machine made of cardboard that was popular when I was in elementary school! Obsessive things, they were, actually coming with coin insert slots and products; you could press a button to get the product out!

Incidentally, as a vending machine maniac, I've bought and created a cardboard vending machine of my own!

That's right—my body is now made of cardboard. In other words, it's now light enough for this number of balloons to support it.

Phew! I made it. Thanks to all the balloons inside my Force Field, my speed of descent decreases rapidly, and I slowly fall toward the ground.

When I saw the Cardboard Vending Machine option in my feature list, I thought I'd never, ever take it. I had no idea it would serve me so well to the point where it saved my life. You really never know where life will take you.

Now that I finally have some time to think, I'll enjoy the scenery below.

The giant circular maze's walls are gray, probably made of stone. The passages travel in straight lines and curves, creating a fairly complex web. I'll record it on my surveillance camera while I can still see the entire thing.

I'm still high up, so I don't know its exact size, but even the narrower passages look wide enough to fit several of me across.

I see it has a plaza-like area and a pond, too. I wonder how much it would cost to make something like this back on Earth.

The stratum I was on before is the Clearflow Lake stratum, and if I remember right, the one below it is the maze stratum. I feel like it had an official name, but Hulemy kept calling it the maze stratum, so it's all I can remember.

She said this stratum is fairly troublesome and very difficult, instinctively disliked by hunters. Naturally occurring treasure chests exist inside, so you can get rich quick here, but there are also a lot of enemies and traps. Plus, the roads are a maze, so apparently more than a few hunters have starved to death after losing track of which direction they were traveling in.

I'm looking down at it from above, so I can see exactly how evil this intricate maze really is.

Ah, looks like I'm landing soon. If land on top of a wall, nobody will come to buy my products. Wait— Ohhh, the tops of the walls are pointed, making it impossible to climb them.

It looks like I'll land in a larger passage at this rate, close to the wall. Hmm. I don't honestly know what would be correct, so I'll let nature take its course. It looks like I'll come down close to the labyrinth's center.

The passage walls are taller than I thought. They stand dozens of yards above the ground. They're considerably thick, too. They're big as five-story housing complexes, and are what makes this place a labyrinth.

I wobble and float down the side of the wall, and somehow manage to land cleanly. Let's get back to my regular vending machine form.

The floor and walls both look to be made of stone, but there are no seams whatsoever. No lights on the walls, either, so it'll probably get dark really fast once the sun goes down.

This passage looks about 150 or 200 feet long, and it goes for a long time to the left and right. Based on what I could see from above, this is like a main road that travels through the labyrinth's center; maybe it's likely I'll meet hunters here.

It should be easy enough for Lammis and the others to find once they come to get me. It looks like I'll be living here for a while.

Normally no one is eccentric enough to want to save a vending machine, but Lammis will come for sure. I fell from a stratum split, so anyone would understand that normally, things were hopeless, whether you were a person or a vending machine.

Even so, I just know that Lammis will come for me.

I have a debt to Director Bear, too, and if the Menagerie of Fools wants me on their team, they'll probably be aggressively searching for me. They might even offer to help Lammis under the condition that she joins them.

If she tries to do something reckless, Hulemy should stop her. I want her to come save me, but on the other hand, I don't want her to force herself too much. I know it's contradictory, but that's what I feel.

First off, thinking about how to survive here is my first priority. There's always a chance that other hunters will come along and rescue me.

Great, then I'll start by inspecting my surroundings. I only got a quick glance, so a careful investigation will get me information I'll need to survive.

I'm currently near the wall of a large passage. The path extends to the left and right, but it goes too far for me to see the end. They're both straight paths, but several smaller ones appear to branch off from it.

At the moment, I haven't spotted any monsters. From my bird's-eye view, I saw some fairly large ones here, but I don't think there was anything in this big passage. Maybe this is a safe zone in the maze.

Anyway, the thing I'm most worried about is the coin with the eight-legged crocodile picture on it in front of me on the ground. It was still in the Force Field when I fell here, so it got brought down as well.

What a dilemma—the coin looks valuable, but I can't reach out to get it. If someone I've never seen before comes along and takes it away, all my products would heat up so much they'd be burning hot.

I want to get it somehow, but as a vending machine, I can't do anything. Sigh. For now, I'll go back over my abilities and points for survival purposes. During my fight with the eight-legged crocodile, I used up a lot of the money we robbed from the thieves.

[Vending Machine: Boxxo]
DUR 200/200
TGH 50
STR 0
SPD 20
DEX 0
MAG 0

PT 1,020,698

{Features} Cold Retention, Heat Retention,
   Omnidirectional Vision, Hot-Water Dispenser (Cup
   Ramen Mode), Two-Liter Support, Candy-Roll
   Vending, Paint Change, Boxed-Item Support, Vending
   Machine Surveillance Camera, Oxygen Vending
   Machine, Magazine Vending Machine, Gas Vending
   Machine, Cardboard Vending Machine
{Blessings} Force Field

With this much durability and toughness, I shouldn't break very easily. I think my speed will increase how quickly I dispense products and warm them. I'll have to experiment with that later.

As for other changes... Hmm? Is this a bug? My point display doesn't quite make sense. One, ten, a hundred, a thousand, ten thousand, a hundred thousand, a million... A million?!

Wait, I, uh, um, whaaat?! Why do I have a million points? I don't recall doing anything illegal to get them.

What's that all about? I get points from exchanging coins, right? I thought that's what the explanation said. The message said I could get points from money. Let's check again.

[You can convert 100 yen to 1 point.]

Right. It says here I can exchange money for points. But—it doesn't say there isn't any other way of gaining points.

What if points are originally things you get from beating enemies? In video games, you usually get experience points or skill points when you beat them. Maybe exchanging money with points is the anomaly here, and you're supposed to defeat bad guys to get them.

In that case, all these points came from defeating the stratum lord, the eight-legged crocodile, which makes sense.

I see. There are ways to get points other than using up money. The more you know—but I don't think I'll have another chance to kill monsters. The stars happened to align this time, but that'll never happen again.

I suppose it continues to be more realistic, as a vending machine, to earn money instead.

Still, now that I've gotten a grasp on my situation, it's finally Blessing time!

Since I have over a million points, I can acquire a new Blessing. I never honestly thought I'd get such a stupidly large amount of points. I also never thought there'd be a shortcut like this.

Well then—let's go over the Blessings very carefully and choose one.

New Powers

First, I separate the Blessings into abilities I need and ones I don't.

Ones like Swordsmanship and Martial Arts are out of the question, since I don't have any arms or legs to use them.

For magic-related ones like Fire Magic and Water Magic, I don't have any magic power, so I get rid of those.

Of the remaining, I'll go over the ones that seem convenient for a vending machine with a fine-tooth comb. First, this one.

Telekinesis—meaning that supernatural ability where you can move things without touching them, right? Let's check the explanation.

[This Blessing allows the user to manipulate objects anywhere within three feet. However, there is a weight limit, and only usable on your own products.]

A radius of three feet—well, that's fine. That's valuable enough on its own. But for some reason, it's limited to my products. Still, if I had this ability, I could do lectures on how to use the products. That's a candidate. Let's check the next one.

[Telepathy]

[This Blessing allows the user's inner voice to reach anyone within three feet.]

This is the one I was after the most. With this, I'd be able to talk to Lammis. It has a small area of effect, but having a rapport with her would still be great.

[Instant Locomotion]

[This Blessing allows the user to instantly move to any spot within three feet.]

Commonly called teleportation. But why is it restricted to three feet? I could only move three feet, but I'd still have a way to move as a vending machine.

These three are the most valuable candidates. However, they're only that valuable if they work the way I expect them to. It's possible they'll consume points to activate like Force Field does.

In that case, I'll have to think about the cost. If Lammis were here, I'd choose Telepathy without a second thought. But I'm all alone in this labyrinth. I hesitate to pick that in this situation.

And in Instant Locomotion's case, I can't help but feel like moving a few feet in this expansive labyrinth would be a drop in the ocean. If I can use it a bunch of times in a row, I might be able to move through the air as well, but that makes me think there's a downside.

Telekinesis is the ability I could use the most effectively as a vending machine. Controlling my products would greatly expand the things I can do. This seems appropriate, but there's no need to rush. I can't spend a million points for nothing.

Come to think of it, if I have this many points, can't I choose a feature, too? I'd thought it would be a while before getting any features above a hundred thousand points, so I didn't ever give them a look.

Still, I think I'll settle on a Blessing, but if there *is* a noteworthy feature— Huh? Was this here before?

[Vending Machine Rank Up]

The way it's worded stirs the soul of a vending machine maniac. Hold on. It's obviously more efficient to choose a Blessing instead. S-still, I suppose I'll look at the explanation, just so I know.

[Vending machines are devices made to provide products and services automatically without the intervention of an employee through the payment of costs such as coins and paper bills. Ranking

up unlocks everything that falls under that definition and also allows for a further variety of optional parts to be attached.]

I can't believe it… In other words, I'll have more features and vending machine types to choose from that I couldn't before? The only things I could choose before now have been things that are actually called vending machines.

Does this mean I could choose features that fall under that definition, even if they're not designated specifically for vending machines?

I'll just have to go with thi— Wait, wait. Calm down. Take a deep breath and calm your mind.

"Welcome. Welcome."

Okay, I'm calmed down. First of all, in this alternate world, and in this maze stratum, choosing a Blessing would be the correct answer. Yes, I understand that quite well.

But think of it this way. I'm a vending machine. I basically got this body out of my love for them. I still don't know why I was reincarnated, but I must never forget that I'm a maniac for vending machines, even after being reborn as one.

Do I want to become a vending machine that can use superhuman abilities? Or do I want to be a vending machine excelling in a myriad of features?

There was never any reason to hesitate to begin with. Yes, I choose this: the vending machine rank up!

[Vending machine rank increased to 2.]

The moment those words appear in my mind, an awesome power… doesn't begin to flow through me. I can't feel any change at all. If I'm rank 2 now, does that mean there are other ranks above that? This is getting a little exciting.

The warmth leaves my body, and now that I'm calmed down, I have a thought: Did…did I actually do that?

W-well, getting stronger and more useful are both important. But I'm a vending machine. If I forget that, I'd be putting the cart before the horse, wouldn't I? Things were inconvenient before, but I've been getting by this whole time.

Yep, that's right. In every choice, you have fewer regrets if you fail by choosing a future for yourself than if you fail by choosing a compromise.

That's enough self-reflection! I decide to get a new feature right away now that I'm rank 2.

My white body stretches into a slender form, and though it—of course—has a coin insert slot, a snakelike hose is attached to my side, and its tip has a plastic material stuck to the end.

It also has a gun-like trigger on it, and when you hold it, a strange *vrooooo* sound comes out and it sucks in the air. Furthermore, there's a switch near the trigger, and when you press that, it expels a gust of air. A fine product.

It looks like it works perfectly—this coin-operated vacuum cleaner in that self-service car wash.

As I explained, out of all the coin-operated vacuum cleaners, I like this variety in particular because not only can it suck, it can blow air back out as well. With it, you can blow out the sand buried in your car seats.

Here's where the problem begins. I know now that I can freely control whether it sucks or blows. What I need to do now is repel the hose's tip outside the Force Field.

When the hose's tip is forced outside the barrier, it comes to a stop on the ground. This vacuum cleaner's hose is easily over five feet long, so I can get it outside.

After that, I blow out air—stop! A little more, make it a little stronger… Oops, that time it was too strong. Blow another short burst of air, adjust the positioning slightly…

As a result of over ten minutes of combat, I manage to bring the hose tip into the ideal position. That's right—so it's right next to the eight-legged crocodile coin.

The hose is all set! No obstacles! Beginning suction!

The suction begins to echo, sucking in dirt on the ground as well as the air. My actual goal, the coin, seems unable to fight against the surprising force. It inches toward the hose, then disappears inside.

Mission complete.

I can feel the coin rattling around in the hose. Come to think of it, what happens to the coin after this? I believe this vacuum cleaner has an exhaust vent in the back; it's positioned over a garbage bin so that the garbage falls right in.

[Octo Croc Coin added to inventory.]

What? Wait, an inventory? I don't remember an entry like that. I doubt, therefore I try it immediately. Let's check my abilities.

[Vending Machine: Boxxo – Rank 2]
DUR 200/200
TGH 50
STR 0
SPD 20
DEX 0
MAG 0
PT 18,595

{Features} Cold Retention, Heat Retention,
   Omnidirectional Vision, Hot-Water Dispenser (Cup
   Ramen Mode), Two-Liter Support, Candy-Roll Vending,
   Paint Change, Boxed-Item Support, Vending Machine
   Surveillance Camera, Oxygen Vending Machine,
   Magazine Vending Machine, Gas Vending Machine,
   Cardboard Vending Machine, Coin-Operated Vacuum
   Cleaner
{Blessings} Force Field
{Inventory} Octo Croc Coin

Oh, I have an inventory entry now. Other things interest me, such as the vast decrease in points and the rank 2 display, but first I'll check my inventory.

[Octo Croc Coin. Proof of defeating the stratum lord.]

That's it?! Wait, no other explanation? Is this a collector's item? Or is there some kind of important meaning behind this coin? I don't know, but there shouldn't be any harm in keeping it.

…Can I get this coin back out? Even if I could, I won't right now, since it takes forever to suck it up. That stratum lord must have been called the Octo Croc.

My points are down to less than twenty thousand, so I can't do anything reckless anymore. And the coin-operated vacuum cleaner actually consumes two thousand points? Many of the features I can choose now that I'm rank 2 cost quite a bit. I'll have to be more careful.

I've done what I needed to do, so I've calmed down a fair amount. Well, whenever you do that, reality comes right after you. For now, I'm in an easy-to-find spot in a stratum, so I suspect there's a high chance some labyrinth-conquering hunters will find me.

The problem there is whether they'll be good people like Lammis and the other residents of Clearflow Lake. It wouldn't be that strange if a band of thieves or some other villainous type came along and destroyed me or whisked me away to parts unknown. There's no guarantee they'll be customers.

I have to consider the worst-case scenario. First, I'll secure enough points to maintain a Force Field. It would be great if I had some other way of getting points. If I can maintain my points, I don't have to worry about shutting down.

Which means I'd have to hunt monsters…which I obviously can't do. I only defeated the Octo Croc out of sheer luck. If you told me to go do that again, I honestly wouldn't want to. At all.

If nothing happens, and I just have to keep my features running, I can hold out for a year or so, but there's no telling what will happen in this alternate world. And yet, the moment I give thought to, for example, why I poured all my points into that rank up, I'll have lost.

[Vending machine form-change time exceeding the two-hour time limit. Please return to original vending machine immediately. Repeating. Vending machine form-change time exceeding the two-hour time limit. Please return to original vending machine immediately—]

What?! Alarms suddenly went off in my head, and now I have this message here. Form-change time limit? Wait, th-think later—by *original* it means the one I'm usually in, right?

I return to my usual vending machine form that instant, and the alarms and warning message disappear. This is a first for me. I suppose it means that forms other than my original one can't go above two hours at most per day.

I've changed my form several times before, but come to think of it, I always have a weird sense of discomfort when I'm in a different one, so I always go back to my usual one. Guess I've never been another vending machine variety for over two hours... I didn't even realize.

Two hours per day is the limit, huh? I should probably stop changing forms without a good reason.

I've been doing nothing but rely on Lammis and Hulemy lately, including with things like this. I thought vending machines were convenient tools where you could buy whatever you want without an employee being around. This is a good chance. Let's take a gander at just how far I can go by myself.

New Encounters

Ah, what lovely weather.

The sun's rays shine down from the heavens, and I bask in tranquility.

Three days have passed, and not a soul has come by. But I'm not the least bit concerned. Just relaxing in the sunlight is bliss.

Before, I might have had a nagging fear in the back of my mind over the thought of my points decreasing ever so slowly. But right now, my points are going up.

The reason has to do with the thing on my head. I added a new feature—a solar panel setup, like the kind on diagonal roofs. With this, I don't have to do anything on sunny days to accumulate points.

See? I told you ranking up was the right choice! But there's no one around. What am I making excuses for?

This solar panel was apparently part of an energy conservation and disaster countermeasure. Mine is fairly advanced, and if the weather is good, I get ten points an hour. If I save up points on sunny days, I can relax and go on living.

For these past three days, to gain a better understanding of my abilities, I first investigated the two-hour limit on my form changing. I learned that I can maintain the form I had when I was reborn for as long as I want. I was pretty sure of that already, but in addition, most exterior changes stuck, and changing any internal features didn't have a time limit.

In other words, even if I devote half my body to the instant ramen function, it doesn't fall under the time limit.

If nothing happens, all I have to do is wait out my time in peace. H-hmm. Once you solve one problem, you start to get greedy.

To put it bluntly, I'm bored. Maybe it's because I got too used to my vending machine body, but I can't really calm down unless I'm selling things to someone.

There really seems to be no human presence in the maze stratum. I wish I'd asked Hulemy a little more about it, but it's too late for that. I have no way to ask her to begin with.

Lammis was knocked out. Is she all right? If the old lady who visits me a lot is around, I'm sure she can heal her, but there won't be any aftereffects, right?

Sigh. Everything has been so noisy lately that it's a little lonely not seeing anyone for an entire day. Giant walls stand in front of me and behind me, and I can see the sky, but that's it.

I have nothing to do, so as I'm looking around as usual, I catch wind of something moving quietly.

Based on the aerial view I recorded with my surveillance camera, the path to my left should be the maze's entrance. Maybe that means I can get my hopes up. It would be ideal if they came from the stratum above to save me, but I don't mind if it's other hunters.

I just hope they're not mean people.

Something grows steadily larger, and eventually I can make the figures out.

Those are bipedal—small black bears...no, cats? Tanuki? I'm having a hard time identifying their features.

There are four. All are wearing the same leather jacket in bright green. They're not wearing pants, but they're wearing shoes? Their jackets aren't buttoned in the front, so I can see their chests—they have white, crescent-shaped patterns on them. Small moon bears?

Maybe they're the same species as Director Bear. Still, they're fairly small.

Their faces and bodies are jet-black, but their noses are black, too, and their ears stand up, with pink inside. They have whiskers as well, but like a cat's. Which means they're not bears? Well, whatever they are, they're pretty cute. As someone whose love for cats is second only to his love for vending machines, I'm itching to pet them.

B-but what is this cute little team? I'd like to give them a closer look while they're buying something from me, but they don't look like they have the time. They're running for their lives, wearing backpacks.

They're being chased from behind by three monsters with loose skin and pig faces wielding clubs over their heads. The bear cats run forward—they're like a combination of bears and cats, right?

Their pursuers have bodies three times their size, and they're certainly not lacking in the speed department. But one of the bear cats' legs is wounded, and two are supporting that one as they run, meaning they can't widen the gap at all.

The monsters with pig faces plastered on their heads are called hugehog fiends, as I recall. I've heard people in Clearflow Lake making fun of fat people by calling them hugehogs.

There's still distance, but please, get in front of me somehow! If you do, I'll help you out somehow.

"*Vaaahhh!*"

"Go awaaay!"

"Just leave me!"

"I won't leave you behind, stupid!"

Despite their appearance, their cries are guttural, and when they open their big mouths, their faces are scary! I can see sharp fangs inside.

The wounded one must be the one with the drooping ears like a Scottish fold cat. By the sound of its voice, it's female. A slightly taller, browner bear cat than the others is supporting her.

The one snarling as it runs is skinny. The one bringing up the rear is plumper.

They look similar, but they have a lot of visual differences. That aside, they should be able to get to me at this rate. About thirty feet separate them from the hugehogs.

The problem is, how do I save those bear cats? It's time for me to reveal the fruits of the painfully long hours I spent thinking up ways to fight as a vending machine.

I change into a vending machine that has a compartment without a lid, then drop several cans of juice into the compartment. Then I change my paint color to match the wall, blending in with it.

At a quick glance, I'd look like part of the wall. They don't have time to look carefully in this situation, after all.

The bear cats run straight by, and as the hugehogs cross my path a few moments later—juice-splash attack!

I use Force Field and eject the cans of juice outside it. They fly at considerable speed, with three of them striking two of the pig people. It doesn't look like it did any damage at all, but the cans that missed are scattered around, making it hard to move, and now they're looking at me.

Then I deactivate the camouflage and say "Get one free with a winner" several times in succession.

"What's that, *oink*?"

"A labyrinth trap, *oink*!"

Oh, they actually end their sentences by saying "oink." How easy to understand. That means these monsters have enough intelligence to speak. Director Bear and the bear cats do, too, so maybe bipedal mammalian creatures have high intelligence.

"Do you remember a trap here, *oink*?"

While the hugehogs are focused on me, the bear cats gain quite a bit of distance. Now to activate my next trap. Pigs are omnivores, right? I've heard they'll eat just about anything.

I change to the vegetable machine—which just got used earlier—and after releasing the glass display, I push all the veggies out of my Force Field.

"*Oink!* Food came out, *oink, oink*!"

"Food, food, *oink*!"

Without a second thought, they pick it up and start chomping down on them raw. They must have been pretty hungry.

Their backs are turned as they delightedly engorge themselves. They seem to have lost interest in the bear cats, and no sooner do they snatch up the greens in their frenzy than they throw them into their mouths.

Meanwhile, I change into a short vending machine from a children's theme park and make my color scheme the same as the wall.

After observing them for a while, they finish eating everything. Seeming satisfied, they smack their bellies and stolidly stand up.

"I'm full, *oink*."

"Hey, the box that made the vegetables is gone, *oink*."

They look all about, and even when their eyes land on me, they find nothing, since my color is the same as the wall before them.

They're confused, but with their bellies full they seem to have lost their sense of caution, so they go back along the path.

I managed to let the bear cats escape, but they went away, too. Crap. I wanted to observe them some more. I'm satisfied with saving them, though, so I guess that's enough.

Those bear cats sure were cute. They were about child-size, too. But what were they doing out here? For monsters that live in the labyrinth, I didn't detect any bloodlust or fear from them.

They seemed to be enemies of those hugehog fiends, too. They seem like one of the friendly races that live with humans, like Director Bear. They could speak, too, so they might have been good customers as well. What a shame.

Still, despite this being an alternate world, the beast people and monsters all seem like they're based on Earth creatures. But what were those bear cats? I get the feeling I saw them once when I was little, but... what were they called?

It was a really cool-sounding name. I remember it drawing my attention when I was in middle school...

"Are we really going back...?"

"The monsters get stronger the deeper we go..."

"The trap might still be active..."

Oh, I hear the bear cats from before talking.

I'd been watching the direction in which the hugehogs disappeared this whole time, so I didn't notice, but they've gotten close.

I turn my gaze to see the four bear cats, paying close attention to their surroundings as they walk.

Now, what should I do? I can pretend to be the wall, and they might not notice me. But first, I return to my usual vending machine color scheme. This one is about the right size for children to use, so for the bear cats' height, this would be easier to access.

Ahhh, their arms and legs are so short and cute!

"What's that?"

"I don't know."

"Isn't it the trap the hugehogs got caught in before?"

The flappy-eared, wounded one is staring intently at me from a distance. The plump bear cat seems to be waiting in the back, too. The other two seem quite interested. They creep toward me, then easily reach their front legs—er, hands—toward me and poke me.

They're probably just trying to figure me out, the same as I'm doing for them. Just as curious as I'd expect, given their catlike appearances. They surround me and start to sniff me.

I am in heaven right now. I'd love to savor this moment of bliss, surrounded by bear cats, but I can't do that, either. It's such a darn shame.

"Welcome."

"*Vooohhh?!*"

The bear cats all jump back at once to distance themselves. I told you, your cries and faces are scary! I'm sorry, it's my fault for startling you.

"*Vaaahhh!*"

The dark-brown one seems strong-willed, and he opens his mouth wide to snarl at me.

The other two are backing slowly away. At this rate, they'll run away from me. I'll change my form, heat up some *karaage*, and drop it into my compartment. Thanks to my speed increase, they finish warming in a heartbeat.

"It lit up and grew!"

"B-be careful, everyone!"

"Shouldn't we run away? Hey, shouldn't we run away?"

The three in the back are even more scared.

The thinner one must be their leader—he's the one urging caution. The chubby one seems the shyest, backing off behind the others.

Crap, they're even cute when they're scared!

"Wait, is that meat I smell?"

The dark-brown one's nose perks up as he notices the scent.

You usually think of cats as liking fish, but they actually like chicken more. The cat I was raising in my home has a criminal record of swiping

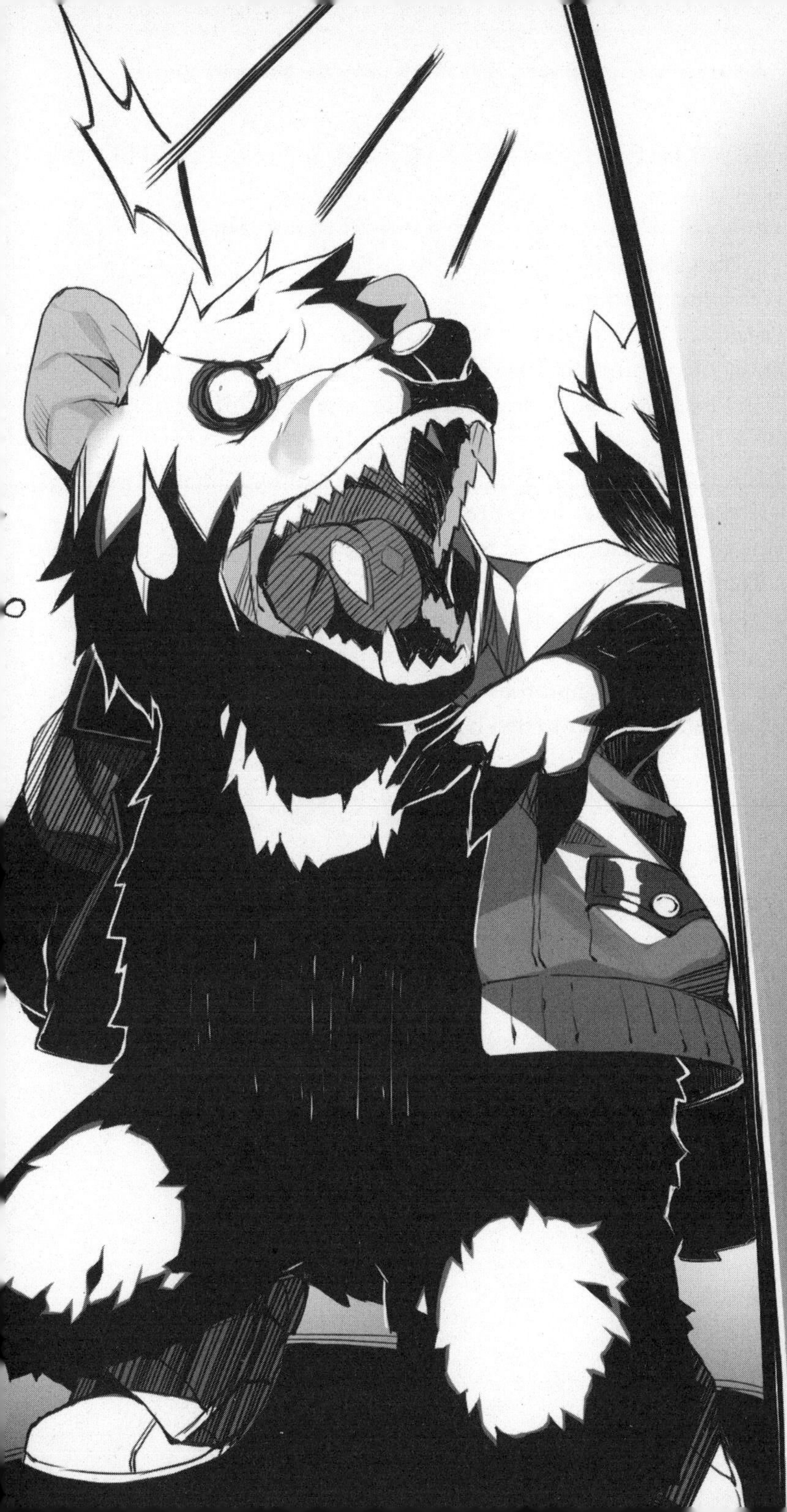

both raw and fried chicken. And even if they're bears, they'll like the meat.

They seem to be making sure that this isn't a trap, but their curiosity and appetites lock them in place.

"Welcome. Insert coins."

"*Vaaahhh...* Ah? Is this box selling things?"

Oh, the flap-eared one noticed!

"Don't be fooled, Suco. It could be the kind that lures you in with items."

The thin one seems the prudent type. Even though the fluffy one is wandering slowly toward me, drawn by the meat.

"Pell, don't get close. Short, you keep your distance, too."

"All right, Mikenne."

Oh, they've revealed all the names of the bear cats. The thin one, their leader, is Mikenne, and the flap-eared female-sounding one is Suco. The chubby one is Pell, and the strong-willed dark-brown one is Short.

Somehow, I have to lure the bear cats into buying something.

The Voracious Devils

They haven't let down their guards yet, but they seem to like the *karaage*. I'd be in a bind if I provided everything for free, and driven by greed, they didn't try to buy anything and simply took the contents out instead.

"Let's just eat them. We don't have any provisions left, and I'm hungry."

Yes, bear cat named Pell, give in to the temptation. Are you the heavy eater character like your appearance suggests?

"Don't be dumb, Pell. Have you forgotten your pride as a pouch-panda-fiend member of the Voracious Devils?"

Mikenne, was it? It's fine that he's puffing out his chest all leader-like, but Voracious Devils? Also, *pouch-panda fiend* is a long name.

According to their name, they have pouches, so I guess they're marsupials with characteristics of bears and cats. Come to think of it, isn't *bear cat* an old Japanese way to say *panda*? And the Voracious Devils... Ahhh! I figured out what animal they're based on! An endangered animal whose cool name caught my middle school self's attention. I think they're Tasmanian devils!

They're cute on the surface, but they have a devilish cry and a white crescent pattern on their chest. I remember now. They're definitely Tasmanian devils. Of course, this is an alternate world, so they could be different, but the haze of confusion in my mind is clear now.

I think I remember Tasmanian devils being carnivores with fairly large appetites. If I can get them to be my customers, I can expect good sales.

"Welcome. Insert coins."

"Do we run, or...?"

"I can't take it anymore!"

Pell pushes Mikenne out of the way and jumps at the fried chicken–filled boxes. He tears into it before the others can stop him, plucks out a piece of meat from inside with steam billowing from it with a sharp claw, and throws it into his mouth.

"Om, nom, *gulp*. It's...it's amazing! What is this?!"

He devours all five pieces in the blink of an eye, then licks the grease off his lips.

"Huh? Is it good? Huh? If you put coins in, you can buy the things on these pictures? Is that it?"

"H-hey, what about ours?! We might as well break open the box... No, I guess we just need to put in a coin, then break the box and get the coin out later. I'm digging in, too!"

"Wait, Suco, Short! This might be a trap!"

Ignoring Mikenne's attempts to stop them, the dark-brown Short removes a silver coin from his jacket pocket, and after somehow locating the coin-insert slot, puts it in there.

"The bumps under the pictures lit up. Does that mean I should press it?"

If he were someone from the settlement, I would respond "Welcome," but they won't know it means *yes*. That kind of exchange has become normal in my settlement life, which is why I slipped up before. It was always more natural for the meaning to fail to get across.

Short nervously presses the button for the fried meats and the product appears in the compartment in a warmed state.

"I thought so. It smells fragrant and whets the appetite. And it's warm, too. I'll try some for myself."

"Me too, then!"

Everyone aside from Mikenne buys the *karaage*, and they chow down noisily on it. They seem to like it. Pell takes out several silver coins and puts them into the slot one after another, hitting the same button repeatedly.

I'm glad I raised my speed stat. At this rate, they might not have been able to stand how long it took to heat them up, and they might have destroyed me.

After dispensing a whopping six orders of *karaage* for Pell, Short and Suco, who were waiting behind him, do the same and buy more.

Even Mikenne, who's been watching me closely with his short arms folded, seems to have reached the limit of his endurance. He wanders over to me unsteadily, puts in a coin, and buys some *karaage*.

"I swear. What are you all going to do if this is a trap? First, we need to taste for poison... *Haah*, the juices are flowing out! What is this? It's amazing!"

Great, they've all surrendered. Now you know the power of Japan's frozen food technology. Wait, I shouldn't act like it's my achievement. Many thanks to you, certain company! Personally, I prefer the fried rice from this manufacturer, but I have doubts these carnivores would eat it.

Still, Director Bear has eaten it several times, so maybe I don't need to worry about that. As I mull it over, I watch them pleasantly...but how long are these Tasmanian devils going to eat for? They've eaten at least one helping each by now, and they've bought twenty already.

Wait, will their stomachs be okay? There really are only four of them, right? To think I'd end up needing to replenish my *karaage* stock just for them—the Voracious Devils are a force to be reckoned with.

"My stomach's fit to burst. And I'm too tired to run away..."

"Come on, Pell. We can't sleep here."

"Can't we take a break here, Mikenne? Suco can't move anymore, either."

"I'm sorry. I don't think I can take another step."

"No, I apologize. I'll stay on the lookout, so you can all rest here."

"Okay. I'll change with you later, so you take the first shift, Mikenne."

Everyone but their thin leader, Mikenne, enters the gap between the wall and me to hide, lie down, and fall asleep within a minute. They must have been really tired.

At this distance, I might be able to protect them with Force Field.

From what I've seen so far, all the members seem to be on good terms, trusting and covering for one another. The thin Mikenne, standing watch, is leaning against me, occasionally losing consciousness. It looks like just standing is a feat for him right now.

It's starting to get dark around here, so you can go to sleep if you want. I'll stand watch in your place. I know those thoughts didn't get to him, but Mikenne, energy drained, slides to the ground and falls asleep.

You did good today. Take a load off and have a nice nap.

"What do we do now?"

"*Mgah, nom, nom, munch.*"

Mikenne is planning the next course of action with his comrades, but they're all intently focused on eating, so they aren't listening. In the end, none woke up until morning, and they seemed to be hungry as soon as they did, so they bought another mountain of *karaage*.

When I took the chance to change forms, their faces hardened and they snarled at me, but once they realized they could still buy their meat, they were instantly fine with the change. Maybe their race prioritizes hunger above all else.

"I wonder what this box is."

"*Gulp.* Phew. A magic item that you can buy food from?"

"Getting to eat such delicious meat was a stroke of luck."

"You seem cheerful, Pell. You know, despite the situation."

As I learned from eavesdropping on their conversation during breakfast, they're not monsters who live in this maze but, rather, hunters. They belong to a certain group, apparently called the Voracious Devils. The name might seem to be at odds with their appearance, but all it took to convince me was witnessing the way they eat.

Anyway, is there some sort of requirement in this world that says hunter groups have to give themselves weird names? As far as I've heard, this maze stratum is fairly profitable but also highly dangerous. Hunters seeking stability stay away from it—which is why I haven't met any other hunters.

The Voracious Devils are, by their own description, "very expensive to maintain for some reason," so they came to this stratum aiming to get rich quick and keep the group together. As for the reason... It's obvious from an outsider's perspective, but… Isn't there some way they can eat less food?

They have high physical ability, too, with their jaw strength and claw sharpness, plus an intimidating Blessing called Roar. They don't seem incompetent as hunters, but since they're born with small bodies, they have trouble handling larger enemies.

But to hear them say it, if there had only been two hugehog fiends chasing them, they're confident they could have managed to beat them without anyone getting hurt, though I don't know if that's true.

After finishing everything, they rub their bellies and lie there in a daze. They're relaxing as though full tummies protect them from any potential threats.

"I have something to say, everyone. Please listen. About what to do now—I think we should try to get back to the entrance somehow."

"But we haven't gotten any treasure."

"I…I agree. We should go back. It's scary here."

"We won't be able to keep the group together if we go back now. Are you okay with that?"

I think your lives are more important, personally. You might want to return. As for the lone female— Wait, I should call her a girl. I recommend you go back once her wounds are fully healed.

"Haven't we already found a treasure? This magic item you can buy food from!"

"Ahh, you're right!"

It gives me a tingly feeling to be called a treasure, but I'm not someone's possession, and I already have a partner in Lammis. I'll voice a word of complaint.

"Too bad."

"*Vaaahhh!* That scared me. I didn't know it could say things besides *welcome.*"

"Get one free with a winner."

"Huh? It can say other things, too?"

"Thank you. Please come again."

I play all my phrases to gauge their reactions.

The pouch-panda fiends huddle up and begin whispering among themselves.

"Did it just react to our voices?"

"I think it was a coincidence."

"But it seems like it was answering our question."

"Do you think the box could have a mind? We'll just have to try."

When they're finished, they all take a step away from me and stare. Their black-eyed stares only serve to give me peace of mind, though.

Mikenne, acting as the representative, takes a step forward, gathers himself, and speaks to me. "Do you actually understand what we're saying?"

That's what I've been waiting for. My answer is obvious.

"Welcome."

"Look, see? It doesn't understand. It's just giving random responses to our voices."

Huh? No, no, no, no! Come on, figure it out. I can't say anything other than those things, and I have to make do with them.

"Too bad."

"Oh, you're right. It's just reacting. It doesn't mean anything. Phew, that surprised me."

"Yep. I'm so surprised I'm hungry again. Maybe I'll try something other than the fried meat."

Whaaat?! No, just try thinking about it again, but harder! You might figure a few things out! I believe in you!

But despite my mental cheering for them, they lose their patience and start eating again.

Sigh… Oh, but I see. Now that I think about it calmly, that was how you'd expect someone to react. It was thanks to Lammis's high intuition that I could communicate with everyone in the stratum, too, but the Devils' reaction is the most natural one.

"Okay, then we'll take this magic item back with us, right?"

"Yep!" "Sure."

The bill has been passed unanimously. I'd like to clear up this misunderstanding somehow, but it's fine for now. I'd be more thankful if they bring me close to the entrance. Once Lammis and the others come looking for me, they'll find me right away.

"Okay. Suco, you're hurt, so the three of us will carry it!"

Mikenne, Pell, and Short go around me and put all their strength into trying to move me. However, they only manage to scrape me maybe an inch across the ground. Every time I run into a situation like this, it reminds me of how amazing Lammis is for carrying me by herself.

"Hhhnnn!"

"Ugaaahhh, vaaahhh!"

"I...I can't do it!"

All three of them fall up against me, breathing raggedly. They may be physically powerful despite their size, but not enough to carry me.

If I go with them, they won't need to secure food, and if it comes to it, I can protect them with Force Field. More importantly, I'd be a little worried if they abandoned me or left me here.

Which means I need to turn into something easier to carry. If I became the cardboard vending machine again, they could probably carry me comfortably. But my restriction won't let me change types for more than two hours. I should save that for when I really need it.

I suppose this here is the only method left. I choose one of the features that appeared after I ranked up, and four wheels appear underneath me.

"Huh? Did it just get a little taller?"

"Look, look!" cries Suco. "Wheels came out underneath the box!"

You noticed? I think it should be possible to move me now, right?

Once again, the members, minus Suco, go around to my side and push, and though it's slowgoing, they begin to move me more smoothly than I thought. It looks like it's a good thing the path here is flat, without any ascents or descents.

"It's moving!"

"We're going to be rich!"

"Will we be able to eat to our heart's content whenever we want?"

"I mean, look at how convenient it is. We could sell it to the Chains Restaurant and be rolling in cash."

I'm sorry to butt in while you're all overjoyed, but I have no intention of being sold. Also, I firmly reject having anything to do with the Chains Restaurant.

Hmm. I bet when they meet Lammis and the others, we're going to have trouble on our hands. It's a distressing thought, but I want to get as close to the entrance as I can, so I'll just push that thought aside for now.

Despite growing wheels and becoming mobile, I still weigh just as much. Pushing me around saps their energy a fair bit, and after an hour of pushing, they take a break.

When that happens, everyone chooses a drink for themselves, clearly thirsty from the effort.

I'd be in just as much of a bind as them if their stamina and motivation ran out, so I provide my products at a cheap price, but it doesn't seem like they need that much in the way of hydration. Compared to how much meat they eat, they only drink as much as a regular person.

They take several breaks over the day, but I feel like we're not really making any progress. I can't see the end of the path, and the scenery around us changes so rarely that I worry we're not actually getting anywhere.

Side paths appear every once in a while, but I know they lead to fairly complicated areas. After all, I have the entire maze recorded on my surveillance camera.

When evening comes, they begin setting up camp early. Karios the gatekeeper has told me before about how monsters get more violent at night, so they must be guarding against that.

That night, I sell just as many products as I did during the day. My morbid astonishment at their appetites has gone into the realm of genuine admiration now. If they had an eating contest with the archer girl, Shui, from the Menagerie of Fools, it could be interesting.

"How much longer until we get to the entrance?"

"About a week at least, I think. It's been two weeks since we came to the maze stratum."

"Well, we got lost for a few days, too. I think that's about right."

"The main road is straight, so I don't think we'll get lost, but we'll run into more monsters. We should be careful."

I haven't seen anything but those hugehog fiends, but I suppose it's only natural that several different monsters live in the maze stratum. Based on what I saw from above, there are giant boulder-puppet things. In regular fantasy works, they'd be magical life-forms created from rocks and boulders—golems.

Also, I spotted something wriggling in the distance, though it was too far away for me to get a good look at it.

"A little farther, and we'll get to where those hugehogs showed up."

"Yeah, you're right. They suddenly jumped out from a side path, and I don't remember much else since they hurt my foot."

"That was really surprising. Just thinking about it is making me hungry."

"Have a little self-control, Pell."

Is this an area where the hugehog fiends wander? Suco's foot has gotten a lot better, so they should be able to run away at full speed if they get chased again.

The Voracious Devils don't know about my Force Field. I know I should tell them about it now, but would they even understand it if I showed them?

If the alternative is hesitating and making a mistake at the last moment, I should show them while I have the chance. All right, let's go for it.

"Welcome."

"*Vaaahhh?!*" cries Suco. "What? Why did this box just talk?!" As always, the cry they give when they're surprised and their super-threatening faces scare the crap out of me.

Everyone's eyes are on me. Okay, let's turn it on for a bit.

"Huh? Huh? What's this clear blue wall?"

"Wh-what's going on? Is everyone all right?!"

Mikenne and Suko aren't currently pushing me, so they're a bit far-ther off, outside the Force Field. The two pushing me realize they're inside the field and panic, trying to get out by hitting their heads on the wall.

"W-we can't get out! Mikenne, Suco, heeelp!"

"Pell, don't lose your head. Stay calm."

Pell, one of the ones trapped in here, has completely lost his compo-sure, but Short is calmly trying to settle him down.

"Vaaahhh!"

Mikenne and Suco open their big mouths and snarl, then swing their sharp claws at the Force Field.

But their claws are unable to pierce the barrier, and they simply bounce off.

"Is this box doing all this? Then I'll...!"

This time, Short opens his mouth and tries to bite me. But I decide Short isn't allowed inside the field!

Short is ejected while in his biting position. He slides across the ground on all fours, glaring at me. He reacts aggressively, totally dif-ferent from his earlier behavior. I'd thought of them more like the Vora-cious Therapy Animals, but it seems like their race can get pretty violent if they need to.

"Vaaahhh! What's the big idea, magic item?! Release our friend!" snarls Mikenne, his expression deadly. The name Devils isn't for nothing.

This turned into something a little unexpected, but in order to clear up the misunderstanding, I decide to release Pell, too.

"P-please just let me out— Oh, I'm out."

"Are you okay, Pell? What on earth was that blue stuff...? And did this magic item do it?"

"Welcome," I say, answering with my usual stand-in for *yes*.

"Are you making fun of us?! What was that 'welcome' for?!" howls Short, enraged, baring his fangs.

Is that how he took it? I guess I can't blame them for thinking I'm making fun of them by saying *welcome* at a time like that. This won't work. I'm too accustomed to talking with Lammis and the others.

In order to communicate with them, I'll need to search for a new solution.

Now I'm frustrated for not having chosen Telepathy, but there's no point dwelling on the past. I'll just have to test and find the best method I can use right now.

I acquire a feature I've been hesitating over called Electronic Billboard. The hesitation comes from its obviously high point consumption. Ideally, it would make it possible for me to display letters to communicate. I'll never know unless I try. Time to turn it on.

A long black sign appears on the upper part where my products are lined up. And then I focus, trying to get letters to scroll across it.

"Welcome. Insert coins. Thank you. Please come again."

I knew it! Just the canned phrases! That was the biggest reason I'd been hesitating. I had a bad feeling that I'd only be able to display what I could physically say. It was so predictable it makes me want to cry.

"Huh? What's that? Weird pictures? Lines? They're going across."

"Are those letters? I've never seen them before."

Oh, right. Plus, they display in Japanese. Well, I knew that part. I knew it would end like this way back when I realized the letters on the cans and my body were indecipherable to others!

I gambled on the last ray of hope, but all this is going to do is display unknown characters to people. Can I get a refund?

Ah, crap. Now what? I'm totally out of options. How am I supposed to make them understand that my Force Field will protect them, not hurt them?

"Does this mean the magic-item box rejects us?"

"Too bad."

"See? I knew it."

No, that's not what I meant, Mikenne. I accidentally said that to mean *no*.

This is such a pain. I miss Lammis and Hulemy.

"We can't touch it. We'll have to leave it here."

"But Mikenne, if we don't bring that back, we'll die of starvation. We don't have money."

"Pell's right. Shouldn't we look for a way to take it back?"

"Yep! We should. Look, it drove us away, but it didn't hurt us."

Oh, maybe there's still hope. First then, I'll turn the Force Field off. And then I'll provide them food again. Here it is—your favorite *karaage*!

"*Hauuu*, I smell the meat!"

"Pell, don't let it tempt you so easily!"

"But you're drooling, too, Short!"

"It might be a trap. I'll make sure there's no poison first!"

I was worried, but they fell for it so easily they're beginning to look like idiots. They pounce on the fried meat, starting their bulk purchasing again. I suppose this means I've won for gaining control over their stomachs.

"*Nom, nom.* There's no way a box that can make such great food can be bad."

"Yeah, you're right. It's delicious."

"Well, it's good. I guess it's all right."

"Yeah, but only because it's good."

Is that all it takes? Aren't you going to, I don't know, vacillate or argue a little more?

Their caution from earlier thrown entirely to the wind, they scoop the fried meat into their mouths handfuls at a time, satisfied as they chew.

When I look at their happy faces, it makes me feel like nothing else matters. I'll probably be with them for a while, after all, and for better or worse, they know about my Force Field now. I'll settle for that.

"*Oooiiink!*"

Suddenly, a hugehog's cry echoes, tearing through the peaceful mood, followed by the thunderous clamor of footsteps heading straight for us. It's coming from the entrance to a side route a little farther down.

"That was a hugehog! Everyone, get ready to escape!"

All of them stand and stoop over. Perfectly ready to flee. Oh, wait, I've seen this before. I'm going to be left behind again. If it means the Voracious Devils will survive, I'll be in charge of buying time once more.

As I watch the spot connecting this road to the side path, six hugehog fiends burst forth. Then they barrel toward us. Sweat pours from their bodies, and they're completely unarmed as they run at full speed.

Wait, why do they look miserable, like they're about to cry? It's almost like they're being chased by something—

As if to confirm my suspicions, the air behind the pigs trembles, and a giant bony hand appears and grabs the wall. It's not just big, either.

It's wreathed in flames, and its intense heat melts the stone wall away, reducing it to magma.

Then a giant skull appears, big enough to swallow one of the hugehogs whole. Just like its arms, its skull is covered in fire, and black flames burn in its eyes.

"That's the Flame Skeletitan! You've gotta be kidding me! Everyone, run!"

The Flame Skeletitan

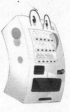

The hugehog fiends seem to just be running away, without any time to attack the Voracious Devils. The Devils, for their part, have already dashed away like hares.

The entire form of the skeleton wrapped in flames is now visible, and it is shockingly titanic. A little more, and it would be as tall as the walls. It must be almost thirty feet high.

The intense heat coming off it is making the view hazy. Every time it takes a step, it melts a foot-shaped portion of the ground that it sinks into. Plus, the vertical vibrations are awful. If it's that big, the bones alone must weigh a ton, considering it's bouncing my vending machine body into the air.

If it's this incredible, I don't think the cola splash we used on the king frog fiend will work. A few plastic water bottles hitting it would be akin to sprinkling water on a blazing firestorm.

I should give up on beating it and think of a way to buy time. The hugehogs should reach me shortly…which means there's only one thing to do.

First, I have to change my form. I add a new feature that appeared at rank 2, a gas pump, and change into that. It's the gas station appliance that's always handy in the wintertime.

The mark of a certain gas station is depicted on my white body, and a sturdy rubber hose and levered nozzle are on my side.

Well, even if gasoline gets on me, as long as I reject it from entering the Force Field, it'll be expelled outside, right? Let's dispense a little gas just to test it.

I pull the lever… I see. As a safety precaution, the gas won't come out when the hose is inside. I should have expected as much from Japanese manufacturing. Mission complete.

No, I'm not a person—vending machine—who would give up so easily. Isn't there some kind of loophole I can exploit?

The Flame Skeletitan takes another step forward and the tremors increase, causing my gas pump body to hop involuntarily. And as I land, the nozzle comes out and falls to the ground.

That was lucky. The tip is aimed conveniently toward the path, too. Let's splatter some gas all over the ground.

The gas flowing from the nozzle begins to wet the ground in front of me. The ground is stone here, too, so it doesn't absorb the gas, instead allowing it to make a thin puddle all through the area.

The hugehog fiends, completely oblivious to what's underneath them in their desperation to get away, step into the gasoline region.

"*Oooiiink!*" they cry, slipping and falling clumsily. Some are clutching their heads and groaning, too. A floor covered in gasoline is as slippery as a skating rink. Now that they've fallen, they'll have a hard time getting back up.

And in the meantime, the Flame Skeletitan chasing after them brings down a giant, blazing foot—and ignites the gasoline immediately, turning my surroundings into a sea of flame.

I have my Force Field up to block the heat and flames, of course, but the hugehogs who fell and ended up coated in gas from head to toe go up in a brilliant blaze.

Unable to even give a death cry, their corpses fall to the ground, and the Flame Skeletitan plucks them up, opens its skeletal mouth, and tosses them inside.

It can eat even though it's a skeleton? Those smoldering pigs are nothing but ashes now—is it okay with that?

Seeing a giant, flaming skeleton devouring burnt corpses amid a sea of flames is more awe-inspiring than terrifying. That's something I can only feel because I'm in a safe zone inside my Force Field. If I were human, I'd probably be paralyzed with fear.

The Flame Skeletitan gives me a cursory glance after eating the six hugehogs, and without coming over to bother me, it walks away.

I'd changed my color scheme to blend in to the wall, so maybe it didn't notice. Or maybe it was full, so it didn't have any interest. Whatever the case, I'm saved.

Still, it left the place in a terrible state. The ground has giant, bony footprints pressed into it, and the walls it got near have melted and resolidified into strange, distorted shapes.

Was that a stratum lord, too? I couldn't see it when I got my aerial view. Maybe it only appears under certain conditions.

Anyway, my only issue now is that I'm all alone again. But I have a feeling the Voracious Devils will come back when they get hungry. Their thought processes seem incredibly lacking. They could have just saved some in their bags for later, but they just ate the food without a second thought.

Also, holes dot the ground in every direction, warped by the heat, so it looks like it'll be hard to push a vending machine.

Even the carefree Devils seemed to sense that this enemy was a direct threat to their lives, and they don't return until it gets dark. Still, as you can see, they do end up chowing down in front of me again.

"Phew. All these surprises really make me hungry."

Pell, you're always hungry.

"I never thought we'd see the stratum lord here... I've heard the rumors, but that was incredible. We'll be able to brag to the director after this."

"That was really, really scary."

"I hear you get a treasure if you beat the Flame Skeletitan, but how on earth are you even supposed to do that?"

I agree, Short. There's no way to beat something like that. It's giant, for one thing, but the flames don't let you get close. Even if you pour water on it to extinguish them, you'd need an entire pond's worth of water for it to do anything.

Throwing plastic water bottles at it would be pointless. I'm out of ideas, so I'll stop thinking about it. I'll probably never fight that thing anyway.

Surrounded by the Voracious Devils as they drift off into relieved slumber, I keep my eyes on the side path the Flame Skeletitan disappeared into.

"Don't go too far right. Left—little more to the left."

They push my body carefully according to Mikenne's instructions. The ground is a mess of holes and hills, so we advance in search of a flat spot. Despite this going on since the morning, the sky is already darkening before we manage to get out of the collapsed area.

We didn't make much progress today, but we'll be on flat ground starting tomorrow, so our speed should increase. If that Flame Skeletitan shows up again, I'll just have to buy them time somehow.

I don't need any more excitement today. I'd like to spend a night in safety.

While I think about this, I'm working overtime as they buy products, one after another. I'm providing them at fairly cheap prices, but I'm starting to worry about their wallets. Won't this put the continued existence of their group in danger?

As always, once they're full, their caution seems to diffuse, and they plop down to sleep without leaving a lookout. Still, I think they'll wake up right away if they sense enemies or hear noises, so if I make a warning sound, they'll jump awake.

It sure is quiet tonight. This wide passage lined with giant walls has a certain atmosphere about it. It's night, so the only light is from my body; a bit farther away, it's pitch-black.

My light is too conspicuous, so I'll turn it off. Darkness settles in completely, and the only thing I can hear is their breathing as they sleep. Ah, it's so quiet it's a little scary. But just having someone else nearby lessens my unease a bit.

If I were human and actually alone here, I might have really gone insane in a situation like this. That's how isolated this place is—it gives me an instinctive terror.

If I had the ability to sense presences or something, it might have been different, but... Oh, come to think of it, there was an interesting feature here. If I remember right, it was around here— There it is, the motion detector.

I could do something like dim my lights at night when nobody is around, then turn them on fully only when the motion sensor picks something up. Oh, but I don't need something like this, do I? I can adjust it all manually when I decide to anyway.

So I thought of a few different things, but watching them sleep that peacefully soothes my soul and makes me not care anymore. Hmm. Being near them makes me feel like their parental guardian.

I have to make sure I, at least, don't let down my guard. I can't see very much in the darkness, so I just pay attention to the sounds. And then I hear something faint.

I locate the direction it came from, eyes peeled, ears ready. It was a small swishing noise, but it doesn't end; it keeps flowing. It sounds kind of like when the heat is on in a stove.

It's coming from the left, a short distance away. I can't see in the dark, but I think I remember that spot being the entrance to a side path.

A faint light comes through the darkness. It looks like it's flickering; maybe it's a lit flame to guide the way. I'd better wake them up.

"Welcome," I say at a low volume, fearing that I'll be overheard.

"Mmm…meat…just twenty more…"

"Mikenne, Short…you can't do that… You're both boys…"

I can hear them talking in their sleep. Also, it sounded like Suco was shipping Mikenne and Short as a couple in her dreams, but I'll pretend I didn't hear that.

They don't seem like they're going to wake up. Wait, I can't leave them like this, so I'll turn it up a little.

"Please come again."

"*Vaaahhh!* Wh-wh-what?!"

I'm glad Mikenne jumped awake for me, but he's too loud.

His shout wakes everyone else up, and they look around in a fluster. At this point, the mysterious source of light must know we're here. It's growing steadily brighter, proving that they're getting closer.

"It's enemies, everyone, get ready to run!"

I have to say, I don't hate their style of choosing escape over battle every time. It's better than a lot of reckless, foolhardy hunters out there.

As the Voracious Devils make ready their escape, a skull wrapped in flames, about the size of an adult human head, appears.

"A flame scoll! We need to deal with it quick, or it'll call the Flame Skeletitan!"

"W-water! Someone hit it with a lot of water!"

That flaming skull is with the stratum lord? If this thing calls it, we'll have no chance of winning. Water—we need water, right? I quickly drop a two-liter bottle of mineral water into my compartment.

"Huh? Water? Water came out of the magic box!"

"We're in luck! Suco, give it here!"

Look, Short, I'd love it if you stopped putting these things down to luck. They don't even consider that I, a vending machine, might have a mind. I think it's about time to figure it out. I drop another plastic bottle off, tinged with resignation.

Once they all have a two-liter bottle, they seem to have trouble removing the cap right away with their claws, so they chop the top part off instead.

All of them charge forward with plastic bottles in hand, moving closer faster than I expected, before splattering the bottles' contents all over the flying skull.

The skull's flames, hit by four helpings of water, go out completely. Without its defenses, Mikenne delivers a bite to the skull, shattering and destroying it easily. When the flames go out, it's pretty fragile, isn't it?

I've only seen them running away before now, so I didn't know their true strength, but they have fairly quick movements. Maybe they're actually pretty strong. You wouldn't think so from their normal behavior, though.

I'm glad we defeated the flame scoll, but they seem to be cautious, watching to see if it called any reinforcements. If the big one comes, they'll have no choice but to run, after all.

After keeping a lookout for a while and making sure nothing else is coming, they decide to take turns standing guard through the night. I hope I can relax a little now while I watch over them.

Reunion

The eventful night passes, and after wolfing down another huge breakfast, they—unusually—begin to make preparations. Typically, they're more likely to laze around until they get hungry.

After experiencing that fight, even the Voracious Devils seem to have learned something, and they stuff mineral water into their backpacks.

"We can beat the flame scolls if we pour water on them, so let's each take one."

"Also, let's take a bunch of food. Whenever we're away from this box, I get hungry."

Pell prioritizes his appetite above all else, but he's right, so everyone nods and chooses products. Meat won't keep, so I line my shelves with sweets and other canned goods that will.

"This magic box is amazing. It has meat when we want to eat meat, and now it has stuff that will last a long time for us. It's almost like it has a mind of its own."

Ohhh, Pell, do you finally understand? Will I be able to communicate with them at last?

"Welcome."

"Nah, can't be. See? It's still only saying *Welcome*."

Mikenne rejects the thought outright, waving a hand in front of his face. Dammit. Next time you buy *karaage*, I'm making it ice-cold.

Sigh. I knew better. If I could say yes and no right now, even they'd figure it out, but *welcome* just won't cut it.

They aren't going to harm me in any way, so I suppose this is enough. For now, my goal is to have them bring me close to the maze's entrance, then get those from the Clearflow Lake stratum to find me.

I do want to give them something as thanks when the time comes. But they might be happier if I lower the prices when they buy an item from me.

"Okay, everyone, let's give it our best today!"

"Yeah!"

Ahh, they really calm me down. We're in danger of monsters sauntering around, but just watching the Voracious Devils makes me want to grin. If I wasn't a vending machine, my face would look awful right now.

They take turns pushing me forward until we spy a raised dust cloud a fair distance away. Is someone fighting? There's too much distance between us, so I can't even make out whether they're people or monsters.

"Hey, it looks like someone's fighting up there. What should we do?"

Mikenne noticed it, too. Everyone stops and cranes forward to look.

"I can't really see it, but I definitely hear fighting."

"Yep, yep. I can hear it, too."

"I think they're hunters. There's a bunch of them."

And I... No, I can't hear anything. They must have pretty good ears.

"What should we do? Join them and help them out?"

"If we do that, won't they steal this magic item?"

"But wait, won't it be hard to get out of the maze alone?"

"Yeah. Getting through alive is what matters. It might be worth it to negotiate, too."

They quarrel for a moment but seem to reach the conclusion that if the hunters fighting are having a rough time, helping them and placing them in their debt would earn them good treatment.

"I'll go ahead and check on them first. We have to see if it's possible to negotiate. You can all take it easy, so bring that closer."

"All right. Be careful, Short."

"Leave it to me."

Short jumps out ahead, and in the blink of an eye, he's tiny in the distance.

We proceed slowly, watching the situation as the three of them push. The combatants are still small as rice grains, and I can only barely make out limbs. I can't tell what they are at all.

"It looks like the hunters have an advantage."

"Do you hear that one making a weird voice?"

"Yep, they're yelling something I don't understand. Is it a girl?"

Making a weird voice while fighting? Maybe they have a unique way of grunting during attacks. Hammer throwers always make their throws while shouting things you can't understand. I hear it lets you put more force into it.

Slowly, slowly, we approach, until we see a shadow rushing toward us at a breakneck speed. I peel my eyes—it's Short.

"Hey, everyone, Director Bear is over there! I talked to him! We should hurry!"

"What? From the Hunters Association in Clearflow Lake?"

"I wonder why he came to a lower stratum."

"But that means we're saved. Director Bear will listen to what we have to say, and the hunters won't steal the treasure we took."

They're all giving expressions of relief as they banter, but I'm just as relieved as they are. Director Bear is here? We're saved…and that means Lammis is probably here, too.

I prepare myself for her bawling or her rage again, deciding to humor her and accept it. It's proof she was worried about me, after all.

"Oh, right. One of those hunters is crazy. It's this human who keeps screaming *Boxxoooooo* and smashing crag fiends with her bare hands."

As I thought, Lammis is with them, too. I must be really worrying her. I'll just have to meekly accept whatever abuse or lecturing comes my way.

"No way! Humans can't break crag fiends with their bare hands."

"No, Pell, it's true. And she's a short woman, too. And she was saying other things as well, like *All he ever does is make me worry* and *I won't be satisfied until I give him a good punch* and stuff."

…If I protect myself with Force Field, she'll probably get mad. Is my toughness high enough? …Maybe I'll increase it some more, just in case.

"Wait, did this box suddenly get heavier? It's hard to move now."

"Oh yeah, you're right. It's really heavy."

It's your imagination.

As conflicting emotions of wanting to see her and not wanting to see her swirl inside me, I'm brought to where they're still fighting.

"Huh? Boxxoooooo!"

As soon as we're close enough to see each other, the hunters' battle ends. When Lammis sets her eyes on me, she begins to run, her feet pounding dents into the ground, charging for me.

Her stomping is breaking the ground! You're coming in too hot! What if I fly away from all the momentum?!

From several yards away, Lammis spreads her arms and slides the rest of the distance. Force Field... No, I can't. If I pushed away a girl crying and leaping at me, I'd be a failure as a man, not a vending machine.

The only option I have...is to take the hit!

I watch her crying face swiftly approach. I-I'll be fine—my toughness is all the way up to fifty. At least, that's what I keep telling myself.

A *thud* loud enough to make the air tremble fills the area, the shock wave born of the collision knocking the Voracious Devils off their feet.

[10 damage. Durability decreased by 10.]

Guhahhh. T-to think ten damage would make it through despite how much I've increased my toughness!

"Boxxo! You idiot! I believed in you! I knew you weren't broken!"

[2 damage. Durability decreased by 2.]

M-my, Lammis, how you've grown. Also, could you please stop banging on me like that?

I consider saying something so that she'll get off me, but when I look at her crying with her tear-streaked face pressed up against me, I decide I need to be silent and endure it.

I have to accept her feelings for as long as she needs to be satisfied.

[3 damage. Durability decreased by 3.]

But I will secretly repair myself.

After overcoming her viselike embrace, she calms down, and the rest of the crew comes running up. A line of familiar faces appears.

"Damn, you made us worry. Phew. But I believed in you, too. I knew you'd be safe." Hulemy puts her forehead on me and hits me lightly with

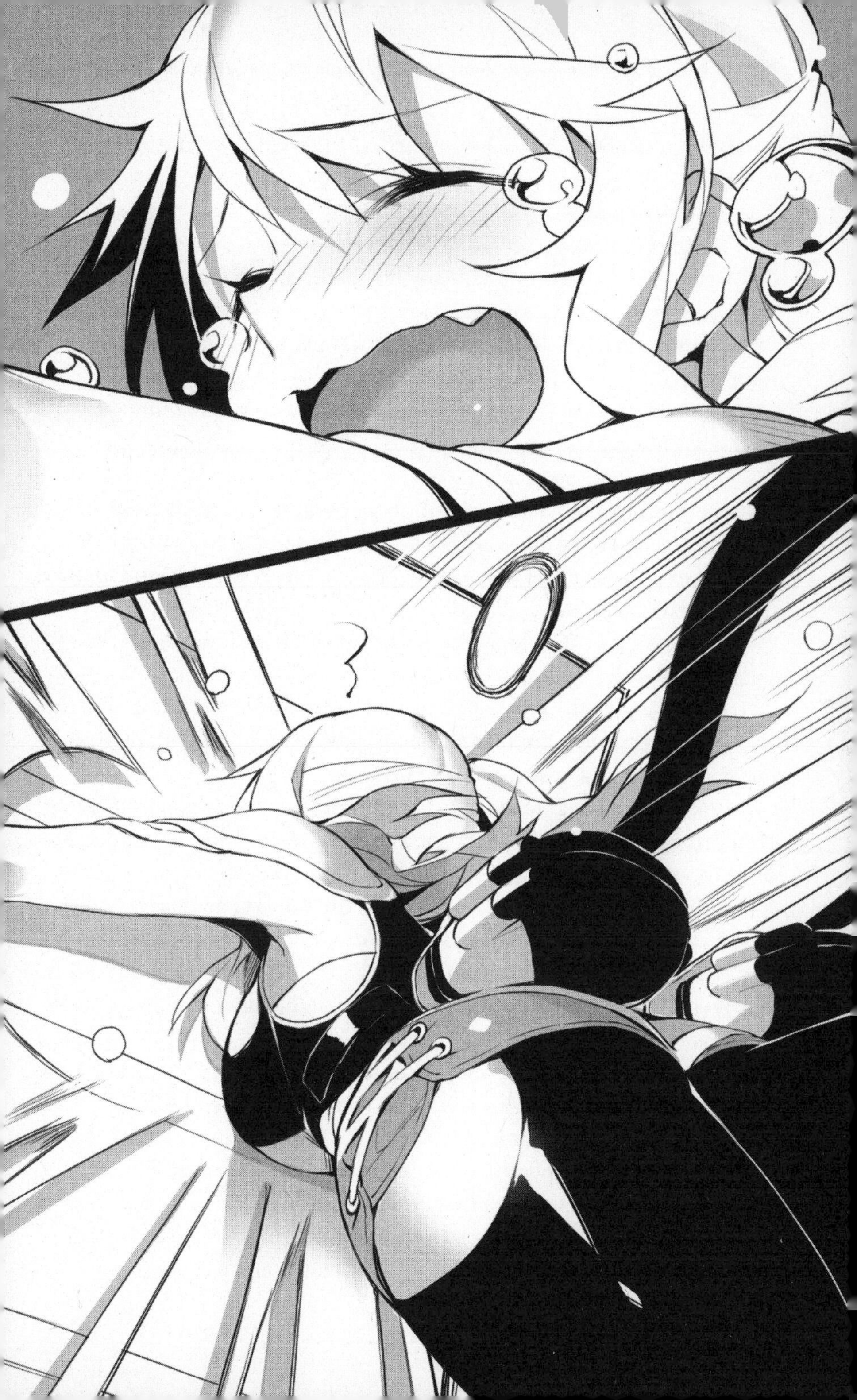

a fist. She must have really been worried—her voice sounds unusually weak.

"We meet again, Boxxo."

"Nothing's broken, I hope. If you broke, where would that leave us? Don't you get it? You even made my beloved girlfriend worry."

The gatekeepers Gorth and Karios came to rescue me, too? Maybe there's a way to ask Lammis to set me up next to the gate next time as thanks.

"Man, Boxxo, are you a sight for sore eyes. If we hadn't found you…"

"That was a close one, huh, White?"

"You're right, Red…"

The men in the Menagerie of Fools breathe a sigh of relief, their shoulders relaxing. Wait, what is this reaction supposed to mean?

"It's excellent that you're safe, Mr. Boxxo. When we told Ms. Lammis that we left you behind…"

"She got super mad at the captain. I wonder what would have happened if we didn't find you…"

After hearing an explanation from the vice captain, Filmina, and the archer, Shui, I understand. Did this girl sitting at my feet, staring up at me, threaten you? I'm sorry for the trouble.

"Boxxo. How is it you're safe? I've never heard of anyone surviving after falling through a stratum split," says Director Bear, looking at me from top to wheels.

Falling from that height would normally kill you instantly. A vision of such a future had occurred to me, too.

"Director, Director, it's been so long!"

The Voracious Devils finally recover from being blown away by the shock wave and surround Director Bear.

"Ohhh, the entire Band of Gluttons is here. Not only did you locate Boxxo, but you protected him as well? You have my thanks."

Hmm? Wait, the Voracious Devils… Are they just calling themselves whatever they want?

"Wait, Director, what's a Boxxo?"

"I can't blame you for not knowing, Mikenne. This magic item is called Boxxo, a resident of the Clearflow Lake stratum."

"A resident?"

The (self-proclaimed) Voracious Devils, aka the Band of Gluttons, all tilt their heads in confusion.

Director Bear sees me, a vending machine, as a resident? I've been too blessed with the people I've happened to meet after coming to this alternate world. Sheesh. I hope no water starts leaking out of sheer happiness.

"Yes, a resident. He lives in the settlement in Clearflow Lake."

"But wait, this is a convenient magic item, not…"

"Ah, right. You must not have realized it. Boxxo is capable of communicating. Right, Boxxo?"

"Welcome."

"But Director, all it ever says is 'Welcome.'"

"Boxxo can only say a few different things. *Welcome* means yes. And *Too bad* means no."

The Gluttons don't seem to believe Director Bear's explanation, and they look at me through narrowed eyes.

"Um, Boxxo, right? Was the first thing the Voracious Devils ate the fried meat?"

"Welcome."

"Okay then, is my name Short?"

The chubby one is Pell, so that gets a "Too bad."

"N-no way. Wait, then you could understand everything we were saying?"

"Welcome."

Their jaws nearly hit the ground, and their perfectly black eyes widen so much they might fall out.

Well, they never thought even for a moment that it was possible to communicate with me.

Their shock, having convinced themselves that they'd be receiving a great sum of money as a reward, is significant, and Director Bear continues his explanation, but they're not listening anymore.

Ah, right. I'll give you *karaage* for free later as payment for carrying me, so will that be enough for you?

Operation and Subjugation

"Boxxo, I'd like a word with you. Have you the time?"

There was no time between the reunion and evening, and as everyone assembled at one side of the main passage and began to make camp, Director Bear came to me.

Oh, that's right. About the Band of Gluttons—they seem to have accepted Director Bear's offer of a special reward, and they're sleeping happily now, bellies full of fried chicken.

"Welcome."

Lammis and Hulemy are on either side of me; they've finished eating the food they bought, and now they're looking at me closely.

"Yes, you two may listen as well. Our first objective of this mission was to search for you, Boxxo. Today, we accomplished that objective."

You did me a big favor. Please, take any product you want for free after this.

"We have the option of returning now, but we actually have a second objective in coming to this maze stratum. It's both an obligation of the Hunters Association director and a request from the Menagerie of Fools."

It being a request from the Menagerie of Fools is within expectations, but what on earth does he mean it's the obligation of the Hunters Association director?

"First, the request from the Menagerie of Fools is to put down the maze stratum's lord, the Flame Skeletitan. My own obligation as director is to investigate abnormal occurrences on the strata. The lord of the Clearflow Lake stratum already appeared—the Octo Croc—and we now have reports of the Flame Skeletitan being spotted on this stratum as well."

I was right—the Flame Skeletitan is the stratum lord here. I witnessed the brunt of its intimidation and overwhelming strength firsthand, so it makes sense to me. I also understand why the Hunters Association would make an investigation. But the Menagerie of Fools are the ones thinking of taking it down?

"The Hunters Association hadn't considered killing it, but the fact remains that the stratum lord's presence ruins the labyrinth's balance and greatly escalates the death rate among hunters. Truth be told, I would personally like to defeat it, if possible."

I get it. Typically, if you ran into that thing, your only choices would be to run or to die. Director Bear's logic in taking action out of consideration for hunters' safety makes sense. I even think it's quite noble for a higher-up to act that way.

But with how the Menagerie of Fools does things—safety first—I don't think we'll be in for a foolhardy battle.

"I believe allowing the Menagerie of Fools to tell you of their objective personally would be for the best," says Director Bear, turning around. The captain and vice captain are standing behind him.

Captain Kerioyl gives me a quick hand wave with his usual lax attitude, and Vice Captain Filmina bows deeply.

"Great, I'm gonna have a seat."

"Excuse us."

Director Bear slides to the side and the two of them sit down directly in front of me. Their usual antics take a back seat to their unusually serious gazes upon me.

"I'm sure you heard from the director, but we want to slay the stratum lord. And we want to borrow your power to help."

You say that, but I don't understand why you would go into such a reckless fight, nor what you expect out of a vending machine in the first place.

"Right, that probably sounded sudden. Well, you know how we call ourselves the Menagerie of Fools? We didn't just come up with that on a whim or anything. We really are a group of fools, an odd bunch you could call reckless."

The edges of his mouth are twisted upward as he talks; it might be my imagination, but his wry grin looked like it was crying for a moment. Vice Captain Filmina, sitting next to him, has her eyes lowered in silence.

"The people in our group have a goal. We already have the mental resolve to do anything for that goal. You may make fun of us and call us fools, or scorn us as eccentrics, but do you know the legend of the labyrinth, Boxxo?"

I've just come to this alternate world, so I would have no way of knowing. I can only respond with an immediate "Too bad."

"The labyrinth… This dungeon, in other words. There are more like it all across the world. It's said that if a group reaches a dungeon's lowest stratum and fulfills the conditions, each of the members will be granted one wish of their choosing. That's what we're after. And to do that, we *apparently* need the coins that drop when stratum lords are slain."

Really… Wait, there's no need to guess—they are talking about the Octo Croc coin in my inventory. I guess that means it's fairly valuable. I wonder how much I could sell it for.

"Rumor has it that you only need some of those coins to have your wish granted. There are eight people in the Menagerie of Fools in all. The twins have the same wish, as do the vice captain and I. Therefore, we have six wishes we'd like to be granted. Right now, we have three coins. Still not enough. And nobody's actually gotten down to the lowest stratum yet, either."

If I use the coin I'm hiding inside me, could I have any wish granted that I want? My dream of a super-high-tech vending machine could be— No, that's wrong. The discomfort of this body has worn off recently, so I'd completely forgotten about it, but it would be possible to go back to being human, too.

"We asked Hulemy, and she said you've got a human soul in there. If you come with us, we can revive you as a human."

I thought he'd suggest that. But it wasn't I who gave an exaggerated reaction to it—but Lammis and Hulemy.

"I-is that true?!"

"I remember seeing something like that in an old document, but Boxxo revived as a person..."

Lammis grabs the captain by the collar, and I see afterimages of his head shaking back and forth madly. Filmina, don't just watch, stop her! His head will come off.

"Get one free with a winner," I say at a loud volume.

Lammis stops. The captain seems exhausted, but he's alive, at least.

Getting any wish granted sounds fake to me, but maybe it's possible in this alternate world. If that's the last hope someone can cling to, then...I can see how attractive the temptation would be.

"Th-thanks, Boxxo. Anyway, calm down. In either case, we have to reach the lowest stratum or it won't mean anything. Right now, we've been traveling the strata to hone our abilities, and when we learn the conditions for stratum lords to appear, we head to their strata to slay them. By the way, Boxxo. There's something I've been meaning to ask you. Did you see a coin when you beat the Octo Croc?"

I could lie here, but I'd like to answer Captain Kerioyl truthfully as thanks for the valuable information. "Welcome."

"So you did. Do you know where the coin is now?"

"Welcome."

His eyes sharpen and a light seems to glow from them. Now that he's revealed his goals, I think I can trust him more than before. He wouldn't betray me while I still had a use to him.

"Can I ask...if you have that coin right now?"

"Welcome."

"I see. That's convenient. Boxxo, Lammis, would you join the Menagerie of Fools—? Well, I'm not telling you to come with us all the time. But when we want to borrow you for your strength or for expeditions, we'd like you to help us."

I'm fine with accepting, for my part, but the problem is Lammis. She's been silent ever since then. When all eyes turn to her, she quickly stands and places a hand on my body.

Then, she smiles gently. "Yep, we'll help! I want to get stronger, too, and I want to be able to talk to Boxxo and eat his homemade food!"

"What am I going to do with you?" sighs Hulemy. "I'll help you out, too. I just know Lammis would fall for some trick or other if she was by herself."

"Our thanks. And we welcome you, too, Hulemy. Anyway, Boxxo—would you lend us your strength?"

Everything's settled into place now, so I only have one answer. "Welcome."

"I see! You being here, Boxxo, resolves all our food problems. Thanks!"

"Thank you very much, Mr. Boxxo. We'll no longer have to suffer through sucking on monster bones due to food shortages..."

Behind the vice captain, who wipes at her eyes in an artificial fashion, the red-and-white twins, who came up at some point, wave their fists in the air, abounded with glee. Next to them, Shui beams and licks her lips. It seems they're more welcoming of me than I thought.

"And just so you know, we want more from you than just provisions, Boxxo. But we're not going to leave you in charge of dangerous spots. We want the kind of help only you can give us in our fight against the Flame Skeletitan."

His words are full of hidden meaning; he must have an idea. He says he'll explain tomorrow, so for today, everyone goes to bed without pressing the issue.

Lammis and Hulemy are leaning up against me, asleep. Sigh. If I had a human body, I might lose my presence of mind and get a little excited. I'm honestly not quite sure whether I should feel thankful or sorrowful for having a metal body in cases like this.

Could I have felt their womanly softness if I had a sense of touch? Well, I should refrain from lewd thoughts about two people who trust me completely.

Still, the captain seems completely intent on killing that thing. How does he plan to do it? He said he'd be borrowing my strength.

The most appropriate plan would be to use water. But I don't think we can do anything with a few plastic bottles' worth of water. He must have another plan... It may be imprudent of me, but I'm almost looking forward to this.

I don't know if it'll be of any help, but I'll think up some plans of my own.

As I sell my wares to the red-and-white twins standing watch, and after they switch the two gatekeepers, I spend all night thinking of a way to slay the monster.

"Everyone ready? We're moving to the spot we planned on. Show me the map you have."

Aside from the predictable development of the Band of Gluttons and Shui seeing who can outeat the other, we find morning quiet and safe. As we're taking a rest, Director Bear speaks.

They spread out the map they got, but it's sort of gangly and imprecise. When I compare it to the image I snapped from above, I can't call it an accurate map by any stretch.

If only I could share my surveillance camera image with them. Is there some new feature I can take? Hmm… What about this? It costs…quite a few points, but I've accumulated a ton of silver coins from the Band of Gluttons, so it should be fine. I choose an LCD panel from the features list. While they're earnestly looking at the map and conversing, I start to test it.

The display is attached to my front side, and instead of actual products lined up, the panel displays them, allowing you to buy them through a touch screen, it seems. Hmm, yes. But can it display the things I've recorded on my surveillance camera in the past?

I'll try everything I can. First, I'll replay the camera video like I always do so only I can see it. And then, I strongly will it to project onto the screen on my body.

Show up, show up, show up, *haaahhh*!

"Ahhh, why are my girlfriend and I there?! I-is this an illusion?!"

The gatekeeper Karios, whose eyes were wandering, sees me and freezes at the sight of the video on the LCD panel.

"It hurts me so much to leave you that it feels like my body is being torn to shreds… But I have a job to do. I'm sorry."

"No, I don't want to part with you, either. But it would pain me if I got in the way of your work. I will fight back the tears, and…"

"Stop, noooo!"

Incidentally, I'm currently broadcasting a recording of their flirting. Is it embarrassing to see it from the outside? Karios squats down and puts his head in his hands. It really does seem to be making him miserable, so I switch the video.

"Is this...the maze stratum?! Boxxo, what on earth?!"

"It's like we're looking at it from far above. Is this...? Boxxo, can you project things you've physically seen? If this is from when you fell from the stratum split, it would make sense."

Things go so smooth with Hulemy here to understand instantly. "Welcome."

"I—I knew it, too."

Lammis, you don't have to get so competitive. It's cute and heart-warming how you're folding your arms, but now's not the time.

I pause it while the entirety of the labyrinth is visible and display it on the panel.

"To think the entire labyrinth would be solved... Boxxo, this is an amazing feat. I'll add a bonus reward for you as director of the Hunters Association."

"Filmina?"

"Understood."

Director Bear nods several times in admiration. Vice Captain Filmina takes out some paper and begins to draw a map from the image.

Hopefully, this will make the maze stratum a little easier to handle.

Secret Plan

"In any case, I have a plan regarding how to slay the stratum lord, the Flame Skeletitan."

As I sway to and fro on Lammis's comfy back, I bend my ear to Director Bear's explanation.

"A large trap waits down this main passage, and there are many hunters who don't know it exists. It's a unique trap that only activates under certain conditions."

"Weight, right?"

Captain Kerioyl slows his pace to move from the head of the pack to us, interrupting the conversation. Is he bored?

"That's right. Anything over a certain weight will trigger the trap…a giant hole. A pitfall, in other words. Dropping the Flame Skeletitan down there will be our contrivance."

If that thing can fit, it must be a pretty big hole. I feel like everyone would notice something like that, though.

"The unpleasant part of this trap is that it doesn't allow people to congregate in large masses and push their way through the stratum by force. The main passage is the origin for conquering the maze stratum. Everyone has to go through it, so if too many are on the trap at once, they get flipped right over."

"That's why we have quality over quantity, right?"

Oh, I see. That's why the two gatekeepers are coming with us, too. After all, Karios and Gorth have excellent skills among the guards.

"The Clearflow Lake stratum has seen an influx of hunters, and its stratum lord is already slain. Karios and Gorth being away from their post will not be an issue."

"They're skilled enough that I'd want them for our group... Relax, Director, I'm kidding."

Director Bear turns a short stare on the captain, who shrugs back.

Calling the two gatekeepers the core of the settlement's defenses wouldn't be an overstatement. Director Bear is in charge of the Clearflow Lake stratum, so them leaving would cause trouble for him.

I think those fears are groundless, to be honest. At the very least, Karios wouldn't ever leave that stratum. I glance over at him.

"Once this is all over, my girlfriend is throwing a welcome-home party. Man, it's tough to be loved, eh?"

Saying that with a broad grin? Your stern, skinhead face is melting. As long as she remains at Clearflow Lake, Karios will remain its gatekeeper. This must be a very exceptional case, so I'll have to thank him.

Next to Karios, Gorth puts a hand to his forehead and sighs. As usual, I don't envy him his situation.

"We're almost to the pitfall. Everyone, get along the right wall. Press your backs up to it."

Everyone obeys, leaning up against the wall and forming a line. Only Director Bear proceeds, one hand to the wall, seeming to grope about for something. After a short time, he nods deeply and looks at us.

No sooner does the ground rumble than a single massive fissure appears to split it in two. Excluding the area right next to the wall where we are, the entire ground of the passage has completely disappeared.

The giant square hole that suddenly appeared looks to my eye like you could fit a whole eighty-foot-long pool in there. The hole is too deep to see the bottom. All I can see as I gaze in is a black abyss.

"The edge is slanted like a mortar, so take caution. I want you all to memorize the location of this hole. I purposely triggered the trap this time, but normally, as long as we aren't all on it, the pitfall will never open...though I have my doubts about Boxxo."

I am pretty heavy. But I think Director Bear is, too.

He manipulates something again, and the ground's lid closes up slowly.

"To be safe, proceed without touching the part of the ground that just opened. Once we're past it, I'll explain the outline of this mission in more detail."

The Band of Gluttons seems scared out of their wits at the hole's depth, but watching them go along with their eyes transfixed to the ground is adorable in its own right. When they're not snarling, they're practically therapy animals.

A short distance away from the hole, we sit down in a circle, and this time, it looks like Captain Kerioyl is in charge of doing the explaining.

"Great. So now that we've joined back up with Boxxo, I'll give you all the details. The hole back there is twice as deep as the Flame Skeletitan. The plan is to guide it above the hole and drop it in, but I doubt the fall alone will destroy it, even if we do things right. And if we attack it from above the hole, its hellfires will melt everything. The idea, then, is to use the vice captain's water-based magic and Boxxo providing even more to fill the hole with water."

I see. That's why you needed me. His idea is that if we can just extinguish its flames, the bones will be exposed like the flame scolls, and we'll be able to damage it. It's certainly possible to put the fire out by flooding the hole with water, but how many hours would it take to fill it?

With bottled water alone, it'll take far more than just a few days.

I've heard it takes half a day just to fill up a school swimming pool with water. Based on this giant hole's depth, it'll take ten times that. Doing it normally would be a dizzying job.

"I know this is asking a lot, but… Do you have any way to sell large amounts of water or discharge it?"

Everyone's eyes gather on me. Those expectant eyes on me make me uncomfortable. If we're talking water vending machines, there are some that sell only mineral water. I believe it was in the features list. But it would take far too much time to fill the hole up with the water I could put out from that.

Water, water… Maybe I can put together the features I've already acquired to come up with something to lead me to a solution.

Come to think of it, if I use the ice vending machine I got before to dump ice in, it might fill up faster than putting in water.

Also, I just added a coin-operated vacuum cleaner from the feature list, too, but that won't do much now. I do remember going to a self-service car wash before, but...hmm? A self-serve car wash. Which means I should be able to choose *that*, right?

Great. I feel like I've been spending far too many points lately, but a vending machine's purpose is to be useful to its customers. I'll add this feature.

By choosing it, my form begins to change. I morph into something several times wider than a vending machine, and several buttons appear. A hard, black hose affixes to my side, and beyond that, a nozzle with a lever resembling a gas pump.

"Yet another form I've never seen. Boxxo, this is your answer, right?"

"Welcome," I answer immediately to Captain Kerioyl's question. I'd normally doubt they'd figure out how to use this, but this time, Lammis and Hulemy are here for me. I trust that they'll manage to do something.

"Excuse me, then. A bunch of bumps—will they respond somehow, like when you press the bumps to buy items?"

"Hulemy, there's a really nicely drawn picture here. Could this be how to use it?" asks Lammis from my side as she points, as Hulemy's already taken her first step in consideration.

Yes—this type has several different courses, and the photograph shows the process and how much it costs. If Hulemy looks at this, with how well she understands things, she'll figure it out.

"Heh, what's this? When a woman holds this, it shoots water! Boxxo, do you mind if I try it?!"

Hulemy presses me, eyes sparkling brightly. I don't have any reason to refuse her. "Welcome. Insert coins."

I've been doing free community service a lot recently, so I appeal to money. The Menagerie of Fools will end up fronting the bill in the end anyway, so there should be no problem.

"Oh? Then I'll pay. Vice Captain?"

"How very like you not to consider paying from your own wallet."

Vice Captain Filmina takes a gold coin out of her wallet and inserts it. Power fills my body, telling me that the preparations are complete.

"Great, all set. Just press this switch, point it away from others, and pull!"

Water erupts from the nozzle's tip, scattering into a spray and hitting the wall. It seemed to be stronger than Hulemy anticipated, because the force made her take a step back.

"Incredible. You could easily extinguish a flame scoll with this."

It looks like she's starting to have fun, since she sprays the water on the wall from the top to the side, starting to clean off the dirt on it.

Lammis and Pell and Suco of the Band of Gluttons watch. Shui and the twins of the Menagerie of Fools go over to Hulemy, waiting enviously, with eyes as pure and innocent as a child who just spotted a toy.

"We can take turns," says Hulemy as though instructing children. She's met with a chorus of yeses. This pressure washer is actually fairly fun to use when washing your car. I've had machines clean the whole thing before, but ever since learning how fun it is to wash it yourself, I've been going for the self-service washes.

"With this much water, filling the hole isn't a fantasy anymore. That's a great help, Boxxo!"

I don't feel *bad* that Captain Kerioyl praised me, but even with this amount, it will take days… No, maybe over a week would make more sense. If I keep shooting water that whole time, will things really go that well?

Plus, is this really the deciding factor? There's no end to my questions and concerns, but if this is really the best option, I'll just have to go with it. Time for me to let loose with everything I have.

Uh, wait, hold on. I can only use a form change for two hours per day… What should I do?

Two days passed after that.

Our days consist of one person wearing a rope just to be safe and fiddling with the trap-activating mechanism to open the big hole, while I keep pouring water inside.

Still, in the end, I'm only a pressure washer for one hour per day in case of unexpected accidents. After that, I continuously drop two-liter bottles of mineral water.

At first, they would have someone open the cover and they'd pour water onto the slanted part inside, but after seeing me getting rid of just the plastic bottle once so the water inside could get out, they immediately understood. Right now, I'm dumping entire plastic bottles down the hole.

Hugehog fiends and risen skeletons appear several times during the process, but it's reckless of them to challenge this many skilled hunters in one group, so we drive them off in the blink of an eye.

When flame scolls appear, Lammis puts me on her back, and whoever we decided beforehand is on water-shooting duty strides right up to them and happily blasts them with water.

With this much water, their flames go right out. They seem to be having fun with it, and when a flame scoll appears, everyone that's not on duty gets jealous.

"I'll go down and check how much water accumulated. Be sure to hold on to the rope."

The lightweight Mikenne ties a rope around his stomach, then has his friends lower him slowly down into the hole. It feels like there should be quite a bit of water down there now, but what does it actually look like?

After a while, Mikenne returns—having been fished out by Lammis—and delivers his report to Director Bear and the others.

"It's cold like midwinter in the hole, but it looks like the bottom has good drainage. The water is seeping into it, so not all of it filled up."

"Hmm. I see."

"I thought it was a good plan, too... It should be effective to drop it down there, still, but I guess we have to go back to the drawing board."

Director Bear and Captain Kerioyl trade looks and groan about it.

Good drainage? There might be something to test here.

"Oh, Boxxo changed all of a sudden. This is— Oh, I get it. If it's cold, we should drop ice in, rather than water."

That's right. It'll only be for an hour a day, but it's better than doing nothing. And I increased my speed, so I can drop the ice out at a much faster rate than before.

Extinguishing the Flames

After that, whenever midnight came, I changed forms and manually dropped a lot of ice in. My speed is increased, so it bursts out like a waterfall.

The hole is apparently fairly cold, and Mikenne, who dangled inside again to make sure, said it's not melting at all.

Hulemy mounted a wooden slide-like object to my compartment, so now I can drop it into the hole without hindrance.

I work in the middle of the night because of my two hours per day restriction, so if I do it during the final two hours of the day, as soon as the date changes, my form-change time limit is restored.

Therefore, my midnight work is generally a one-person job. Lammis and the others said they would wake up for me, but I politely declined. In that case, they should just stand watch normally.

If the Flame Skeletitan has the same characteristics as the flame scolls, as long as we put out its fire, attacks will get through. But I can't help but feel that with only water or ice, it would vaporize them in an instant.

"Boxxo, what are you thinking about?"

As I straddle the date and return to my original vending machine form, Lammis pops up from behind.

Still, why does she know when I'm worried about something? I should be the same vending machine as usual.

"Maybe you don't notice, but whenever you're thinking, your lights blink and get weaker sometimes."

Really? I hadn't noticed at all. Lammis is very observant.

"Boxxo, can I ask you something?"

Unusually, her smile disappears, and a serious gaze falls on me. This doesn't seem like a situation where I should poke fun or play dumb.

"Welcome."

"Boxxo, do you want to go back to being human?"

That's a hard question. Normally, you'd want to go back to being human instead of staying a vending machine. Even if you *are* a vending machine maniac...

At first, I hoped to go back to being a person, too. I still have the desire to go back to being a person so I can exchange words with Lammis. But then I realized something. If I went back to being a person and was no longer a vending machine...would I have any value?

Right now, I feel that I'm helping Lammis and the rest of them. But if I went back to being a person, it would mean going back to an average person with no particular redeeming qualities.

When I think about it, I get scared. If I go back to being human, I'd probably be happy at first. But in the back of my mind flashes a future where everyone eventually knows I'm useless and says they liked it better when I was a vending machine.

And I'm even anxious about whether or not learning Telepathy will break the illusion when I talk to her. I was never very good with words when I was human. Would I be able to have satisfying conversations with them? Would they be disillusioned after talking to me, saying I'm not a very interesting person?

Maybe, back then, I unconsciously avoided taking Telepathy for that very reason. I have the bare minimum communication ability that I need already, so I forced myself to believe that was enough, and let go of my chance to talk to them.

It's pathetic. How can I have more confidence in my existence as a vending machine rather than a human?

"Get one free with a winner."

"You mean you're not sure? One day, I want to talk to you and do all sorts of things with you, Boxxo. Oh, and like I said, I want to eat your homemade cooking, too!"

If I had arms, I could embrace her and her unyielding smile. If I had feet, I could walk shoulder to shoulder with her, rather than be carried around on her back.

Maybe that alone would be enough. If that is her desire, then I will live my life with that as my goal. No matter what the result is in the end.

Several more days passed. There's a good amount piled up in the hole, too, so we're apparently going to carry out the operation. The gist of it is that we locate a flame scoll first, then maneuver it to this pitfall.

Then, with the pitfall closed, it calls the Flame Skeletitan. Once it's above the hole, we activate the trap, drop it into the hole, and when its fires go out, we launch an attack from above.

To do that, we start loading the cart full of rocks. The main battle force for this is Lammis.

The rocks aren't that big, though, which bothers me. Lammis could carry much larger boulders, but apparently the buar cart wouldn't be able to hold the weight, and there weren't any bigger ones anyway.

It's tough, not being able to say anything about things you haven't tried yet. As long as we trap it in the hole, the danger will be less for the time it can't climb back up to us. I would think just that fact would put the attackers at an advantage.

"Captain, it seems Red has made contact with a flame scoll," explains White to Captain Kerioyl with a hand over his ear.

"Great. Have him lead it this way."

If I recall, the red-and-white twins know a special Blessing that makes it possible to talk to each other no matter the distance, though they can't talk to anyone else. Despite the restriction, it must be a convenient skill. Obviously, the captain would value it.

"You heard him. We'll wait a short distance from the hole. Mikenne, put on your hooded mantle and get to your assigned position."

"Got it."

Mikenne, completely covered in a mantle the same color as the wall, takes up his position in front of the pitfall's activator. When he turns his back, it looks like he melts into the wall. Unless you pay close attention, you might not realize he's there.

We lie in wait in position on the other side of the hole. Now we just have to buy time until the scoll calls the stratum lord, then execute the plan.

"Boxxo, be honest—how does this look to you?" asks Hulemy in a hushed tone, bringing her mouth close to me. "Think we can pull it off?"

I think times like these come down to luck, but it's less about whether I think this will go well and more that I *want* it to.

"Welcome."

"I see. I really want it to work, too. But the rumors say that the Flame Skeletitan's flames are strong enough to instantly vaporize water. I wonder if filling the hole with ice will be enough..."

Ah, I see. That's what Hulemy is apprehensive about. I'd like to clear away her worries, but I don't possess a way to tell her.

"Red is almost here!"

"The Menagerie of Fools will be on duty waiting above the hole. Don't let go of our ropes!"

"Leave it to us, Captain!"

"You may rest easy."

Lammis and Director Bear grip the ropes tied around their waists. Also, the captain's is tied around my body. I wonder what would happen if I changed forms... I'm curious, but I'll restrain myself.

Red bursts out from a side passage with three floating flame scolls in pursuit. He fished up that many?

"We can beat up to two of them—but make it seem like we're having a difficult time. Be sure to leave one."

"Roger that!"

The Menagerie of Fools pounce on them in high spirits. With their skill, the flame scolls will never get the better of them, so I can watch without worrying.

They do actually handle them with room to spare, so now we just have to wait for the guest of honor—the stratum lord—to appear. As the flame scolls numbers dwindle to one and the Fools whittle it down slowly, I feel a faint rumble from the ground.

It looks like our real prey has arrived. I can see the air trembling in spots connected to a side passage. It must be the high heat creating a mirage.

"Great! You know what to do!"

"Yes!"

The Menagerie of Fools easily take down the last flame scoll, then position themselves in the center of the pitfall. Everyone watches as a giant skeletal hand burning with crimson flames appears. And then its fire-veiled skull suddenly materializes, close to the top of the wall.

"It's already hot from this distance?" Hulemy wipes sweat from her brow, staring intently at the Flame Skeletitan. Everyone's faces are strained. I don't blame them—a giant skeleton on its own is strange enough, but it's covered in flames hot enough to melt the walls.

"You should back up a bit," says Director Bear, urging Hulemy to move a little.

The Menagerie of Fools are starting to retreat as though frightened, but I catch sight of them glancing underfoot.

With every step it takes, it prints a melted, foot-shaped depression into the floor, just like last time. It starts out slow, with heavy movements, but gradually increases its walking speed until it reaches a trot.

It closes in on us with rumbling and ground-melting force; looking at it objectively, it's incredibly disheartening.

"Don't get caught! Run straight through!"

The Menagerie of Fools run like their lives depend on it—well, they do—and the flaming skeleton continues to close in from behind. It swings its arms, and while they seem to just barely be out of reach, the hot winds the swings create blow their hair all over.

"Hot! It's way too hot!"

"Captain, please leave your whining for later."

"No fair, Vice Captain!" pipes in Shui. "You have water covering you!"

"Don't you have any consideration for your subordinates?!"

"I'll take some water, too, please!"

After hearing their shouts, I glance at the vice captain. She is indeed coated head to toe with water. That must be why she's the only cool-headed one there.

But they all have enough presence of mind to engage in witty banter.

Each one gets past the pitfall, and just as the Flame Skeletitan enters it—

"Now, Mikenne!" roars Director Bear.

"Right!"

Mikenne, disguised as the wall, activates the trap.

The ground underfoot disappears, and the Flame Skeletitan, its hand outstretched, disappears from sight.

"The steam is going to come out, everyone!" shouts Hulemy. "Don't get close to the hole!"

The members trying to sneak a peek immediately stop what they're doing.

But no matter how much time passes, no vapor erupts from the hole, and everyone's gazes gather on Hulemy.

"H-huh? The water should be evaporating... What's going on?" Hulemy groans, unconvinced, folding her arms.

Mikenne's curiosity gets the better of him, though, and he nervously peers into the hole.

"Hey, everyone, the skeleton's flames are out!"

"I don't get it, but if they're gone, great! Start throwing 'em in!"

By Captain Kerioyl's barked order, everyone begins throwing huge rocks inside.

I'm probably the only one who knows why the flames went out. I was dropping something into that pitfall, but it wasn't ice—it was actually dry ice.

Dry ice is a mass of hardened carbon dioxide. When the Flame Skeletitan fell inside, the dry ice melted and filled the hole with CO_2.

That much is taught in elementary school physics, but if fire doesn't have oxygen, it can't burn; and carbon dioxide is heavier than oxygen, so it collects underneath—where its flames are, in other words.

It's a good thing it worked, but if it had failed, it would be too horrible to look at. This was an independent decision I made, so I'm seriously relieved.

Now, then. It would be great if we can just exterminate it like this, I hope against hope as I watch them drop stones in one after another.

The Finishing Blow

"Mikenne, how does it look?" asks Captain Kerioyl as Mikenne peers into the hole.

"It looks like we've hurt it some, but I think we still need another push."

The smaller stones haven't quite done the trick, huh? If they used something heavier and harder, it might work... Hmm? Why is everyone staring at me right now, I wonder?

"Wouldn't Boxxo do the trick?"

"Wait, but if we fail, Mr. Boxxo will break."

"He fell from a stratum split just fine, didn't he?"

Captain, Vice Captain, would you please stop with all this dangerous talk right in front of me? Still, to be honest, changing into a giant vending machine and falling on it kind of seems like the most effective option.

"You can't! I won't let you put Boxxo in danger!"

"There's no guarantee. I'll have to oppose this, too."

Lammis and Hulemy stand in front of me as if to protect me. I'm happy they feel that way, but if this plan is our only way to deal a decisive blow, then I think you should consider it.

I've gotten quite a few more points of toughness, so I think I should be fine if I fall. As long as my durability doesn't reach zero, I can repair using points, so I think I can do it. But if it doesn't work, it's all over for me.

"Right. Boxxo's been such a big help in the past. It would be cruel to ask any more of him. And we have to strut our own stuff, too."

"Shall we jump in and kill it in one fell swoop?"

"Well, as long as the flames aren't in the way, we could…"

Wait, no, no, you can't do that! The bottom is filled with carbon dioxide. If you go down there, you'll have trouble breathing—actually, you'll die from carbon dioxide poisoning!

I didn't expect this. I have to somehow get them not to go down there.

"Welcome. Welcome. Welcome."

"Oh, Boxxo, you agree."

Nooo! "Too bad. Too bad. Too bad."

"You don't? But if we dally too long—"

"It's trying to climb up!"

Well, it didn't have any reason to sit quietly in the hole. Of course it would try to climb up. Now we have even less time. But I can't let people go down there.

"We can't pass this chance up. You ready, everyone?!"

"Please don't let go of the ropes!"

"Seriously, please!"

"Seriously, this is no joke, after all!"

Their gung ho attitude in times like these is worthy of respect, but this is absolutely the wrong time! They can't. At this rate… Don't I have some way—some way of stopping them?!

My current position is a short distance away from the hole. It's about ten feet to the slope on the edge of it. Lammis and Hulemy are close by, as are the Band of Gluttons, excluding Mikenne.

The captain unwraps his rope from my body, then hands it to Director Bear. He'll be better if they need to adjust the length.

Isn't there some way to bring my body to that sloped edge? First, I quietly attach wheels to my bottom. Now if someone pushes me, I should make it.

Even if I had a way to tell Lammis what I wanted to do, she would no doubt refuse. Hulemy doesn't seem like a good bet, either. Which leaves Director Bear and the Band of Gluttons.

If the Band of Gluttons were to push me, they'd all have to combine their strengths to move me at all. Director Bear's hands are full with the rope the captain left him with. Of course, Lammis's Might seems more than capable of giving me a light push to propel me to the slant.

Oh...I just thought of something. However, to do it, I'll need to throw away my shame and reputation. But this is to win. Lowering my affection level with them is better than them dying.

I select a form change—to a porno mag vending machine.

"Wait, Boxxo, you changed suddenly... *Wh-whaaat?!*"

The lasciviously dressed women lined up behind the glass are in seductive poses, a feast for the eyes of those with such tastes.

When Lammis sees them, her face goes red in the blink of an eye. "*Hyah*, eh, why are these people in their underwear and sticking their butts out and lifting their chests... *Uwaaah!*"

Even though she's blushing hard, her eyes are fixed on them. She seems like she's curious despite her embarrassment. I know the feeling, Lammis.

But this isn't the time to be reflecting on how moe the embarrassed Lammis is. Time for a little insurance.

"Welcome."

"*Heauhh!* S-stop it, Boxxo. I'm not buying any of these. You pervert!"

Because my greeting broke her concentration as she was trying to collect herself, Lammis overreacts, and in order to conceal her embarrassment, she slaps me.

Normally, it would only make a light sound. In her frazzled state of mind, however, she must have underestimated the amount of force she used, and the impact on my body is monstrous.

And thanks to that impact, my vending machine body quickly slid to the side. If not for the wheels, my body would have only shaken, but for my current state, her force was more than enough.

"Huh? Boxxo?!"

"Thank you."

Panicked, she reaches out, but her hand only grasps air while I accelerate toward the slope, hurtling toward the hole.

As I sense my body has come off the ground, I then change into a giant vending machine.

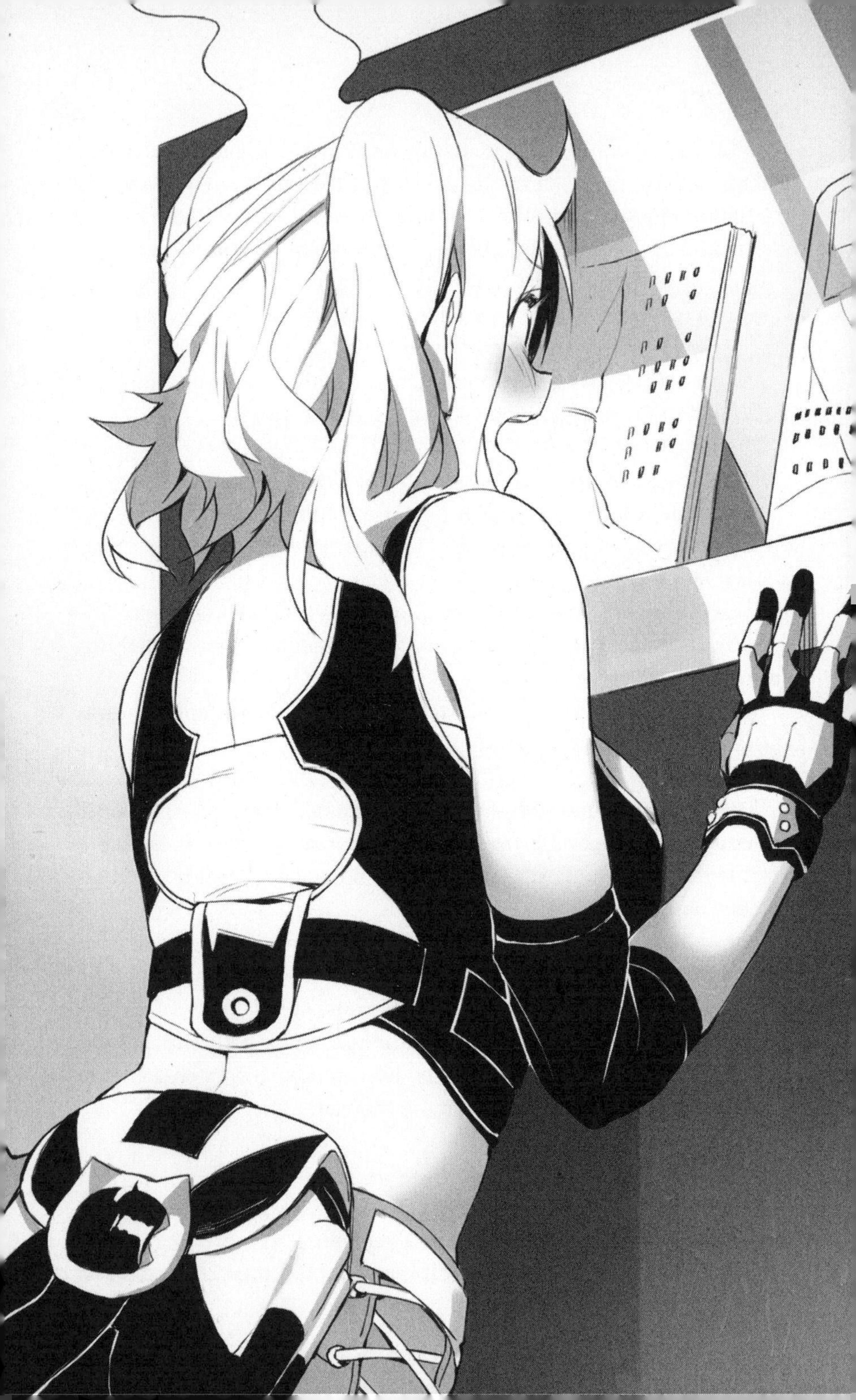

When I look down, I end up staring the skeleton in the face as it tries to clamber out of the hole. It will fall into the hole if it lets go, and a vending machine is now falling toward it from directly above.

Let go to bat me away, or take the hit? The Flame Skeletitan hesitates for an instant—at the cost of its life. It must not have been able to make up its mind, because I strike it square in the forehead, my vending machine body easily shattering its skull.

It was fortunate I struck at the right angle. After smashing the skull, my body destroys its throat, its rib cage, and its hip bone before plummeting to the ground.

[12 damage. Durability decreased by 12.]

The damage is less than I thought, probably because crashing through all the bones broke my fall.

A third of my body ends up buried in the ground, which looks pretty uncool, but all's well that ends well.

Bone fragments clatter down from above in a rain. Looks like I finished it off properly. All is well.

"Boxxooo! Why are you always so reckless?! I'm coming down now, so wait a second!"

Lammis is infuriated. She seems like she'll descend right this second. Wait, it's still filled with carbon dioxide down here, so I'll change into an oxygen vending machine and release oxygen.

"Too bad. Too bad. Too bad."

I say *Too bad* several times in a row to warn her away, but she doesn't seem to have a mind to listen as she throws a rope down from above the hole. I'll continue my high-speed oxygen flood!

My constant shouting seems to have an effect, though, and Lammis hesitates to descend. Maybe people around her stopped her.

"Boxxo! Do you mean it's still dangerous down there?"

"Welcome," I respond immediately to Hulemy's question. Times like these make me thankful she's around. Lammis is quick on the uptake, too, but as soon as I'm involved, she gets reckless.

I'm glad she's worried, but I wish she'd worry about herself a little more. Of course, I guess I'm not one to talk.

Come to think of it, we defeated the stratum lord, so wouldn't there be a coin dropped somewhere nearby? Oh, there it is. Like last time, I use my coin-operated vacuum cleaner and manage to adjust it to suck up the coin.

The item Flame Skeletitan Coin is added to my inventory.

Now I just have to keep expelling oxygen for a while... Wait, if oxygen is lighter than carbon dioxide, it wouldn't mass on the bottom of the hole. In that case, it's time to show everyone how I survived that stratum split.

I create a load of balloons, and when my Force Field is full of them, I become a cardboard vending machine. My body is enveloped in a floaty feeling, and I start to flutter upward.

Since I'm inside carbon dioxide right now, I think the relative weight is making it easier to float. I rise more quickly than I thought I would.

After getting a bit more than halfway up the hole, my speed decreases dramatically. That must be the line under which the carbon dioxide is filling. I made more balloons than last time, so my body still manages to go up.

"Um, Boxxo?"

"Welcome."

I was worried I wouldn't be able to speak as cardboard, but it seems fine. Well, the other vending machines can't replay voices, either, yet I could talk now.

"Mikenne, close the hole, please."

"Yes, sir."

At Director Bear's order, the hole's cover closes. I turn off the Force Field, release the balloons, and land. Then I return to my usual form and breathe a sigh of relief...when a shadow falls over me.

I have a bad feeling about this. I don't want to look, but I can't pretend not to know, so I reluctantly look ahead.

Lammis has her hands on her hips. She's leaning forward and puffing out her cheeks. Yep, no mistake. She's mad.

"Boxxo, what would you have done if you broke?"

Her gentle voice is, conversely, scary.

"Get one free with a winner."

"Don't beat around the bush. I'm steamin' mad right now!"

Yikes. When she gets riled up, her accent comes out. I'll just shut up now.

I don't have the conversational skill to persuade women anyway, so with the voice data I have now, nothing I can say will change it. That, however, was a foolish idea, I think to myself an hour later when her lecture ends.

At first, she was angry, but then it evolved into her complaining and saying how worried she was. It continued until eventually Hulemy can't bear to watch anymore and stops her.

"Lammis, leave it at that. If you blame him too much, he won't like you anymore."

"Aw. Okay, I'll stop here. Just don't do anything reckless ever again, okay?"

I answer her entreaty with silence. I don't want to lie to her, so I can't answer her. If we encounter a situation where I can save everyone, I would probably do the same thing.

She doesn't grow angry at my attitude, though. Instead, she gives a pained grin. Almost like she can read my mind, and she's fed up with the result.

"Is your talk over? I have a question as well. Do you mind?"

Captain Kerioyl, evidently having watched for the right timing to speak up, lets his finger crawl over his hat brim and walks over.

"Good work again, Boxxo. Did a coin drop from the stratum lord at the bottom of the hole?"

"Welcome."

"Oh, great. We should go down and get it."

I guess I'll give them the coin I picked up. Um, how should I do it? I look at the Flame Skeletitan Coin entry in my inventory, then will it outside...

"Whoa, you got it for us!"

The coin falls to the ground in front of me just like I wanted it to. The captain doesn't hesitate to bend over for it, but an outstretched hand grabs his arm from the side.

"What's this about, Hulemy?"

"You seem to be trying to take it as though it's yours. But Boxxo is the one who beat the Flame Skeletitan and picked up the coin. You don't have ownership of it."

Her argument is correct, but I don't really care either way. Still, maybe it's better to do these things properly than make friends.

"Right, my bad. It's true—because of all you did, we pulled through. Without a doubt, it's Boxxo's right to take it. Instead, I'd like to buy it from you. How does a hundred gold coins sound?"

You can't give a that kind of price with such a carefree tone. A hundred gold coins converted to points is a hundred thousand. Wait, that's a ridiculous fortune!

Lammis seems just as surprised as I am, looking between the coin and me with wide, round eyes.

Hulemy doesn't seem particularly shocked, and she glances over at Director Bear, who has settled in as an observer.

"Hmm," he says. "The market price for stratum lord coins certainly is around there."

"See, Boxxo? What do you say?"

In that case, no problem—in fact, that would be great. I've already secured one stratum lord coin, so I don't need any more.

"Welcome."

"I knew you'd understand, Boxxo. This will be quick. You don't mind if we pay at a later date, right? We can't exactly walk around with riches like that."

The deal is made, and the coin becomes theirs. Captain Kerioyl plucks the coin and holds it up to the light, and after looking at it closely, he tosses it into a bag at his waist.

Well, then. All we need to do now is return to the Clearflow Lake stratum. My time in the maze stratum has ended with only a bird's-eye view and the main passage, but I don't think I'll ever be coming here again.

Epilogue

"Gee, I still can't believe it," mutters Captain Kerioyl in a voice that one could take as bafflement or admiration, staring at the magic item that was, a short while ago, simply a thing a blond-haired girl carried around.

"Believe what?"

"Running into two stratum lords in such a short period of time, for one thing. But the fact that a magic item with a human soul inside beat them. If we told other hunters, they'd never believe us."

"I agree. Even we have trouble believing it, despite seeing it first-hand," says Vice Captain Filmina, combing her hair up and sighing a little.

"Maybe there's something about Boxxo that draws them near," says Shui.

"Maybe he's actually got the makings of a hero, and this is destiny? Anyone called a hero always gets wrapped up in trouble wherever they go, after all. That's how the stories we heard at home went, right, Red?"

"But those were just fairy tales, White."

The three members speak lightly about it, but the captain remains silent for a moment, watching Boxxo. "You might be more right than you think. The thing is worthy of a checkered fate, isn't it?"

"A soul...," says Filmina, "inhabiting a magic item we've never seen before."

"Yeah. I don't know whether it's fate or a curse, but it could still be a negative Blessing."

In this world, there exist special powers called Blessings. But not all of them are positive ones. Some are equivalent to curses, abilities that bring misfortune to whoever possesses them.

"Well, I don't have proof, but it's a little too well-done to shrug off as coincidence," says Kerioyl. "It may be the devil's luck for Boxxo, but it's real fortune for us."

"You're right," says Filmina. "Normally, you'd think it impossible to acquire two of the stratum lord coins we've been seeking in such a short time."

The other members all nod.

The Menagerie of Fools wander the labyrinth in search of the coins dropped by defeated stratum lords. In these past few years, they've only gotten three. To even see two without a year going by is a first for the captain.

"Maybe it's not Boxxo," suggests Shui. "Maybe something strange is happening in the dungeon itself."

"We had a king frog fiend come up, after all," says White. "Something could be going on."

"Yeah," says Red. "I feel like the encounter rate for monsters has been high, too. Didn't Hulemy mention something about it?"

Shui cocks her head to the side in confusion, and the red-and-white twins do the same, as though prompted by her gesture.

One of the conditions for Hulemy being a temporary member is that the menagerie will give her regular, detailed information on the strata in exchange for her giving them intel and advice regarding monsters. They must be remembering that.

"Come to think of it, rumor has it the Monster King's forces are getting more active," mentions Kerioyl. "Could be one of the factors causing all this shady stuff in the world."

"That may be too far a leap," says Filmina. "The Monster King's forces, though... They were after the bastion in the north of the empire, right? They're apparently managing to hold out, but I hear it's only a matter of time before it falls."

A being that controls the monsters living in the northern wastelands: the Monster King.

The monsters living in those lands have excellent individual ability, but their self-willed attitude leads them to frequent fighting among themselves, meaning they've never had the time to invade other nations—but then, one appeared who forced those monsters to yield by force.

It called itself the Monster King and, with the monsters it bent to its will, began to attack neighboring kingdoms. Their power is great, and one nation has already been destroyed.

The empire is blessed, too, though, for the bastion city sits on the only path connecting it to the Monster King's lands. Though it manages to endure the attacks now, there have been whispers that an imminent fall is plausible.

"But still, who calls himself a Monster King anyway?" says Kerioyl. "You're the king of the monsters—we get it. Such terrible naming sense."

The captain shrugs, failing to see the point, but everyone looks at him as if to tell him "You're one to talk."

For certain, the Monster King would probably not want the captain to tell them that, considering he came up with the name Menagerie of Fools.

"I don't know whether it's a coincidence or if some power is at work, but that Boxxo really gets your gears spinning...," he says. "He might be essential for granting our wishes."

The Menagerie of Fools' eyes all gather to one point.

The vending machine, which Lammis worried over and Hulemy teased, didn't notice their gazes, leaving his mechanical body to its fate.

Afterword

Thank you very much for purchasing the second volume. Boxxo's range of action has broadened a fair bit compared to Volume 1. I was going for a "cool-guy" vending machine. What did you think?

This marks the second time I'm writing an afterword. In the first volume, I wrote about what led me to writing the novel. It ended up being a little heavy, so this time, I'll aim for a brighter afterword.

It isn't as though I particularly liked novels growing up. I was bursting with interest in manga, but I could never read them when I was little.

The way my family raised me was rather strict, and I was forbidden from reading manga or watching anime until middle school. My mother hated all that stuff, so the only anime I got permission to watch were *Sazae-san* and *Doraemon*. (Although I watched other things in secret when my parents weren't around.)

The only manga in our house, too, were historical ones about famous people from Japan and the rest of the world, but starved for manga as I was at the time, I read them front to back, over and over.

Normally, placed in a situation like this, one would concentrate on his studies, but I hated studying with a passion. Then I had the easygoing idea that if I couldn't read manga, then I could just read novels, right? That led to me reading every novel I could get my hands on every day.

They weren't limited to pure literature and the kinds of stories you'd find in textbooks; I mainly read action-adventure novels, historical ones, and books about the ecology of animals and insects. I was reading them as a stand-in for manga, so I remember liking books with interesting stories or ones where I could learn things I didn't know.

That's the kind of kid I was, so looking back on it, there were quite a few odd things about the way I spoke and acted. Whenever everyone else would have conversations about what they'd read in shounen manga magazines, I hadn't read them, so I couldn't keep up. If someone asked me directly, I'd say things like "Anyway, can we talk about Thomas Alva Edison?" I was a weirdo.

At the time, we had a biographical manga about Edison in the house, and being able to say his full name like that was a small pride for me. When I think about it now, I was the kind of kid my friends didn't like too much because I always showed off my book smarts.

When I entered the later years of elementary school, after learning how interesting novels were, I was taken in by short-short stories, began to enjoy stories with sophisticated endings, and dabbled in Sherlock Holmes as well. That was how my twisted, unchildlike personality strengthened.

Once my grade school days were over and I began middle school, my mother suddenly lifted the ban on manga. She told me that now that I was in middle school, I should judge the good from the bad myself. I remember her talking about things like how she raised me the way she needed to in elementary school, and now she wanted me to take responsibility for my own actions.

Then I had a thought. Was this…a clever trap of hers? Was she letting me swim, waiting for me to slip up, get ahead of myself and buy manga, only for her to say how unhealthy the things I was reading were, claim it's harmful, confiscate it, and talk to me about how I should be studying harder? I decided she was.

I was eager not to let her catch me with that one, so I thought about it long and hard.

At the time, I enjoyed watching *Sherlock Holmes, Tuesday Suspense Theatre,* and Western detective dramas, so I had started to fancy myself a deductive expert. I put my skills to work, looking for an answer as to how to go about living in the future.

Continuing to read novels like I always did would be the safest method. On the other hand, my desire to read manga grew by the day. Finally, I had an epiphany.

Couldn't I just read light novels, many of which were fantasy, instead of the regular ones my parents liked? I could just take off the cover and it would look like a normal book. I would skip over pages with pictures on them while my parents were around, then enjoy them on my own time in solitude.

In that way, I enjoyed my days buried up to my shoulders in light novel worlds for my three years of middle school. Incidentally, I understood that my parents really wouldn't get angry even if I read manga or watched anime when I entered my second year of middle school.

Well, after that, I ended up getting absorbed in stories about the human heart, like psychology and multiple personality disorder, when I got to high school. But when I look back, I also feel like that was the height of my youth, or a rather late *chuunibyou* phase.

When I talked to my mother about it, she was proud, and boasted "Well, I guess the fact that you're writing novels now is thanks to me!" She's not wrong, but why do I feel weird about it?

Anyway, if you'd told me at the time that I'd be in a position to let other people read stories I've written like this, I'd never have believed you.

Ituwa Kato not only provided the gorgeous illustrations once again, but also added to the main character's vending machine shenanigans, and those beast people, too... Thank you so much.

My editor M and everyone in the Kadokawa Sneaker Bunko editing department, you've all been a great help on both Volume 1 and Volume 2.

To my mother and older brother—thank you for telling our relatives and your friends about this.

Thank you to my friends who went to the bookstore to purchase this, too.

And to all the readers who purchased Volume 2—I ask for your continued support in the future.

Hirukuma

Suco dreaming of
anthropomorphization.

(Ituwa Kato)

EVERYONE'S FAVORITE SPIDER GIRL RUNS WILD IN HER VERY OWN MANGA!

So I'm a Spider, So What?

Art: **Asahiro Kakashi**

Original Story: **Okina Baba**

Character Design: **Tsukasa Kiryu**

VOLUMES 1-3 OF THE MANGA AVAILABLE NOW!

Visit www.yenpress.com for more information!